SEALED WITH A KISS

WILD CANYON ESTATES STORIES, #3

TE SHERIDAN

Sealed With a Kiss

by

TE Sheridan

Contemporary Romance Novella

Published by TE Sheridan

Edited by A. Marie

Cover Photo: Deposit Photos

Cover by Redbird Design

ISBN#: 978-1-951637-00-2

1

W *ild Canyon Estates Party.*

Evan Bellinger had seen the notification pop on his phone calendar; he'd been watching it get closer every day. It used to be he almost dreaded these nights. He knew most guys would love the free pass to flirt with and fuck other women—younger, older, blondes, redheads, skinny, and curvy, too—but that free pass was for everyone. Not as much fun when your wife was at the same party, doing who knew what with any number of guys that weren't you.

Knowing that it took hooking up with someone else for his wife to get off had been a huge blow to Evan's ego. Janie had been a firecracker in bed back in the day. She was limber and adventurous, and she was always eager to please. But she hadn't gotten the same pleasure out of their sex life that he had, and while he'd known that, it wasn't something they really talked about as a couple. Rather than deal with it head on, they had skirted around the issue for too many years, and Janie had found her sexual pleasure with her fingers or her vibrator.

That was bad enough. But when she'd come home with

an invite to a party at her coworker's house and hinted to Evan that it sounded very adultish and a little risqué and even a bit forbidden, he knew it would be a problem. If that first conversation about the parties had plagued him with dread, actually *going* to that first party had been sheer hell. Janie, with her blond hair and big blue eyes, had taken fifty by storm. She was a knockout when they met; Evan thought she was even prettier with a touch of age and wisdom in her face. Petite and slightly curvy—Evan loved the curve of her hips and her full breasts—Janie had a personality bigger than the state of Texas. She was fun, and her boisterous laugh turned every head in the room.

No question the parties—the sexual freedom—suited her. He had promised her that first night that he was okay with whatever happened; he loved her far too much to begrudge her the pleasure he hadn't been able to deliver nearly often enough. But watching other men want his wife, and watching his wife play with other men had been a hell of a lot harder than he had ever imagined. There were pluses— not even including his very own free pass. Seeing other men come on to Janie had reminded Evan just how sexy his wife was, and with a whole new playground of opportunity, Janie had learned to relax with him when they were alone together at home. But he still thought it strange to say sex with other partners had saved his sex life, maybe his marriage—because who knew? It was possible, wasn't it, that once the boys were grown and gone, Janie might pack her bags and walk out in search of something better?

Watching her with other men would never be easy, but Evan had finally decided when in Rome...Then again, a year into the parties, he still wasn't ready to check his inhibitions at the door. Janie had made it clear to him and other party guests that she had no limits. Many party guests didn't. Evan did. He didn't articulate them, because he honestly didn't know what they were. But he wasn't ready to dive in head-first and put everything out there.

The wedding shower earlier in the summer for Janie's friend Felicia and her fiancé Matt had been kind of fun. Harmless, if you counted your wife skinny dipping and messing around in the pool with other guys harmless. Evan had played the games, though he'd stayed away from strip poker. He'd enjoyed a few rounds of *Spin the Bottle*, and who didn't love drawing dirty pictures for someone else to guess?

He wasn't exactly looking forward to the next party—the one that was this Friday. But the last one had left him intrigued and a little bit anxious to be back at Donna and Frank Jackson's house. Funny thing about that? He hadn't done a thing that was questionable. He'd found a girl he'd kissed at the shower when they played *Spin the Bottle*, and he'd walked her around the backyard for a while. Whitney hadn't been happy to be there; she hadn't been happy, period. They'd flirted a bit, and they'd shared a kiss, but Evan had been content to sit with her and answer questions about how parties like that one affected his marriage.

Which was why he found himself sort of looking forward to Friday night. Whitney might not be there; in fact, if Evan had to guess, Whitney and her boyfriend wouldn't come back. He just hoped they had worked things out. But it had been fun getting to know her, and maybe on the off chance that she would come back…

Janie had called him crazy that night. He was at a free-for-all party, with anything his heart and dick desired on tap, and he chose to while away the hours talking to a girl who was unhappy in her relationship. Maybe he was crazy. He'd been honest with Whitney, teased her with a comment about kissing her breasts and telling her he'd be happy to see her again. In truth, he would have been happy to play around with her in the small alcove they'd claimed out back. His dick had been rock hard all night. No shortage of fun girls there, he had reminded Janie, and one of them had blown him before the night was over.

So, Whitney may or may not be there, but Evan had decided earlier in the week when the party reminder kept popping up on his calendar app on his phone that he was going to have some fun this time. He still had limits, but he still didn't articulate—even to himself—what they were.

He assumed he was alone when he heard the click of the door. He slipped his glasses off and pinched the bridge of his nose. He enjoyed teaching the personal finance class at the local university, but he'd been up too late the night before, and he was paying for it now with a headache. He glanced at his watch and decided he had time to grab a cup of coffee before he headed to the office.

The quick zzzzppp from the back of the room startled him. He covered a yawn as he looked up from the podium where he was gathering his notes and met the eyes of the young woman who sat in the back of the second row. She grinned and tipped her head as she stood.

"Caught that, Mr. Bellinger." She pulled the strap of a worn black backpack over her shoulder and meandered up the row of desks to stand in front of him. Evan hated being called Mr. Bellinger, but last summer when he'd accepted his friend's invitation to teach a personal finance course at the university, he decided having his students call him Evan wasn't professional. Still, a year later, he bristled at the formality. It was a fast-paced class that required squeezing a lot of information into a short time frame—eight weeks—and he'd found that an informal setting worked better. But several students still addressed him as Mr. Bellinger.

"I need coffee," he said now with a laugh. Konnor Horton snorted; her black eyebrows arched so high they kissed her hairline.

"Wow. When your teacher bores himself to sleep…"

Evan gasped and clutched his heart. "I'm not bored, and I'm not sleeping," he argued, still grinning. He hadn't known what to expect when he took the job. He and Janie didn't need the money, although, the extra income didn't hurt. But he liked kids—had two of his own, and he thought it was kind of funny that they were horrified that he was teaching at the university—and he was doing Rob a favor, filling in a temporary—though in year two, it was beginning to feel permanent—need for a finance instructor for the summer term.

Konnor's smile was bold, radiant, but the thought filled him with guilt. He dropped his files in his own backpack and followed her to the door. When he reached around her to open it, he caught a whiff of her perfume—something light and flowery, which kind of surprised him. Konnor didn't strike him as the light and flowery type. She was tall for a woman, with a strong athletic build. Evan had never seen her dressed in anything other than skinny jeans, combat boots, and old, faded t-shirts. Likewise, he'd never seen a hint of makeup on her face.

He liked that. She had a peaches and cream complexion, and her deep green eyes were fringed with crazy long eyelashes. She wore her black hair in a sleek, sexy cut that framed her thin, angular face and emphasized her long, graceful neck. The right side of her hair was perpetually tucked behind her ear, and Evan had noticed a row of sparkling studs in the pale pink shell. All of that together should have made her look hard, unapproachable at the least.

But she had an incredible smile, and she enjoyed conversation. Which wasn't to say she was flighty and needed to hear her own voice. Evan had thoroughly enjoyed having her in his class so far this summer; she was witty and perceptive, and she'd challenged more than one person in the room already, on topics ranging from the national debt to the stock market.

"I don't like talking about credits and debits," she admitted as they walked the carpeted hallway to the stairwell.

"You wound me." He tossed his hands up as if asking for mercy. "What's a guy gotta do to impress a girl like you?"

She snorted and eyed him silently.

"Yeah, don't answer that," he agreed.

"I work in a bank," she explained. "It's mind numbing."

"Why are you in personal finance if you work in a bank? I mean, you're already my star student."

"Getting a business degree," she answered simply. "It's a required course."

"Mmm." He nodded. "So, it wasn't my stellar reputation that attracted you to the class."

She flashed him that bold smile as he pushed open the door to the stairwell.

"Of course, that had a lot to do with it." She shrugged and laughed softly when Evan rolled his eyes. "Don't get me wrong. I like numbers and dollar signs. But I work as a teller. Hard to go back to a job like that."

"Go back to a job like that? What does that mean?"

Evan stepped to the side of the stairs and followed her to make room for a group of girls coming up. They were all dolled up in tank tops and tiny skirts, four of the five in heels that could kill a guy in more ways than one. Evan was surprised when Konnor greeted them warmly.

"I worked at a bank when I was in high school," she told him over her shoulder. "Had some stuff happen and had to quit. Moved here. Came back to school to work on a degree and got a job at a bank. Had to start at the bottom, just like anywhere else."

"Custodian?" He grinned. "You don't strike me as a maintenance person."

She laughed again as she hit the bar on the door at the first floor of the stairwell. Evan followed her out, and they headed toward the main university entrance. Blinded by the sunlight after being inside all morning, Evan squinted and shielded his eyes with his hand. Konnor rummaged around in her bag—still on her shoulder—and dug out a pair of sunglasses.

"I'm a teller," she mumbled. "Which is what I did at the first bank."

"You got hired as a teller when you were in high school?"

"Right out of high school. Worked there through a temporary agency and got hired on after the summer."

He nodded, curious how old she was since she spoke with the disdain that he often heard in his wife's voice. He wouldn't ask, though. Women were touchy about their age; just because Konnor was younger than him didn't mean she wouldn't be touchy about her age.

"Are you getting coffee?" she asked as they skipped down the stone stairs at the main university entrance. Evan shot her a cautious grin, ready for her to rip on him again for being boring.

"I think I have just enough time to grab a cup before I go to the office." He nodded. He could grab a cup at the office, but that meant making his own or drinking the weak stuff his coworkers drank. Might as well drink water.

"You're a real estate broker? Is that right?" She walked beside him around the winding campus path. He eyed her silently, but she was looking at the parking lot, not waiting for him to flinch at her question.

"No."

"No?" She swung her gaze back around to look at him. Evan noted true surprise in her expression.

"I was in real estate about twenty years ago," he told her. "Where did you hear that?"

"I don't know." Konnor shrugged. "So, what do you do?"

"I'm a financial analyst."

"Okay."

"I work as a consultant for a few different clients. Currently working on some numbers for a local healthcare facility and some new software they're considering."

Konnor shivered in distaste. They had reached the campus coffee shop. Evan stepped around her to pull the door open, but Konnor reached for it at the same time. His hand brushed the back of hers. Konnor looked at him over her shoulder, her green eyes mysterious.

"I got it," she said quietly. He offered her a small smile and allowed her to open the door.

"I thought you said you were a business major." He swept a quick glance over the interior of the small shop. Thankfully the line wasn't long; the majority of the tables were empty. Only one girl sat at the bar that ran the length of the window. Two girls were head to head in the corner where the shop sold items with the university logo.

"I am."

From the corner of his eye, Evan saw Konnor shrug.

"What are you having?" He nudged her with his elbow and corralled her up to the counter to order.

"I want to be involved in running a business. Not a person crunching numbers telling people how to run their business."

Evan chuckled. He glanced at his watch as Konnor asked for a large to-go black coffee. Evan leaned around her as he pulled his money clip from his back pocket and asked the barista to make it two.

"People involved in running businesses need number

crunching people testing software and marketing campaigns and feasibility reports—"

"Oh, I know." She watched Evan hand over a twenty to the barista to cover both coffees. "I just don't want to *be* the cruncher. You didn't have to do that."

"I'm happy to do it," he answered simply. He tucked some of the change in the tip jar and wadded the rest to stick in the hip pocket of his khakis. "What sort of business do you want to run?"

"I don't know," she admitted. "My stepfather owns a few restaurants where I'm from. I'm pretty sure I'm not interested in the food industry, but I loved tending bar at his places."

"You tended bar?"

"Yeah. Worked for him for about a year?" She shrugged. "Met some interesting people."

"I'm sure you did," Evan agreed. He studied her profile as she stared up at the giant chalkboard on the wall behind the counter. He'd worked as a waiter for a few years before he and Janie met, and while he agreed with Konnor that the food industry wasn't for everyone, he liked the bar. He'd met interesting people just from cruising up to the bar to pick up drink orders and deliver them back to his customers.

The barista—an impish girl with a bob haircut—handed them their coffee. She flashed Konnor a big smile. Konnor wished the girl a good day, and she and Evan walked back out of the shop.

"So, do you work today?" Evan asked her as they headed back the same way they'd come. His car was in the faculty lot, but he had no idea what Konnor drove or where she might be parked.

"I do, actually. They changed my hours up a bit so I could fit your class in."

"Good." He nodded. "Well. I'm over there."

Konnor grinned and sipped her coffee. "Thanks for the coffee, Mr. Bellinger."

"Please call me Evan."

"Can't." She winked as she stepped by him to head in the opposite direction.

He laughed and took a step, but he stopped when he heard her say his name. *Mr. Bellinger.* Her smile lit up an already beautiful, sunny day when he turned to look at her.

"Get some sleep tonight." She arched an eyebrow at him.

"Thanks." He laughed and shook his head. Konnor nodded and turned to walk away. Evan watched her go, his eyes first on her hair—it shined almost blue in the sun—and then on her ass in the tight-fitting jeans. The exact opposite of Janie, but Evan thought she was cute.

Realizing he was standing on campus watching the sway of a student's hips and picturing her perfect little ass naked, he stirred to life and turned back to the parking lot. Konnor was off limits. It was one thing to look at the women—some of them a hell of a lot younger than him—at the Wild Canyon Estates parties. Completely another thing to undress a student with his eyes.

That could get him into trouble with the university administration. Possibly the law, if she was underage, though Evan seriously doubted that.

But the attraction he felt for Konnor would most certainly get him in trouble with his wife.

2

"Do you have to wear that dress?" Evan mumbled as he settled into the driver's seat of their Highlander. He started the SUV, put it in reverse, and then settled his hand on the back of Janie's seat. He loved the dress, and he loved the high neckline and her bare shoulders exposed, and he loved that under the dress she wore nothing. But he still hated walking into Donna and Frank Jackson's house with her and handing her over to any or every other guy there.

"Really?" Janie laughed, her eyes wide with disbelief. "Does it even matter what I'm wearing?"

It didn't. Not really. But then again, yes, every fucking thing about these parties mattered to him. Janie was right. She could waltz into the Jacksons' house wearing a turtleneck and slacks. But she'd be naked with someone's hands on her within the hour, so no, it didn't matter at all what she wore to the parties.

Still. As much as Evan loved having her dolled up and sexy on his arm when they entered the Jackson house, watching other men ogle her was still a bitter pill to swallow.

"We could stay home," he suggested as he backed the SUV out of the garage. "We have the house to ourselves."

"We'll have the house to ourselves when we get home," she reminded him.

"It's a little much," he argued. "In the same night."

"You don't really want to stay home, do you?" She reached over to rest her hand on his thigh. Evan chuckled when she slid her fingers up under his shorts. "I thought you were having fun at the parties."

"Fun is relative, Janie," he said quietly. He backed the SUV into the street and then headed in the direction of Wild Canyon Estates.

"It's not my fault you're limiting yourself to the occasional blowjob." She patted his leg and withdrew her hand.

"That's not what I meant," he argued, "and I'm sorry I haven't found a woman I want to fuck the same way I want you."

He heard her sharp intake of breath and winced. While the jealousy did occasionally make him green, he didn't doubt that Janie loved him. And there was the fact that she had figured something out that made sex between the two of them pretty incredible. It was unconventional, maybe, but it worked. He didn't want to hurt her or make her feel guilty for finding and celebrating her sexuality.

"I'm sorry," he mumbled. "You know I'm just on edge."

In his peripheral vision, he saw her nod.

"I just wish you would let yourself enjoy what's there." She shrugged.

"I'll be fine, Janie," he promised her.

Several cars were already parked in the street, all the way up into the cul-de-sac at Donna and Frank's house. Evan recognized several, though there were always a few he didn't. There was always a new face or two, and sometimes those new faces interested him. But he hadn't found anyone yet who made him want to fuck her.

The night was hot and sticky, perfectly normal midsummer night for the Midwest. And yes, that made Janie's dress not only sexy-as-fuck, but also practical. Evan slipped his arm around her waist as they walked up the drive to the house. The thump of electronic music rattled his bones before they were close to the door. Evan had wondered what the neighbors thought the first time he and Janie had come to the Jacksons' house. But seeing several of the neighbors at the party put that worry to rest. He'd also seen the faces of a few law enforcement people there as guests, but then, Frank and Donna ran a tight ship.

They served alcohol, yes. But they also had everyone take a Breathalyzer before they left with car keys in hand. They played loud music, but then didn't most people who had parties? Evan and Janie's neighbors blared classic rock at all hours, seemingly for days on end. And sure, a lot of intimate things went on at the Jacksons' house, but it was all behind closed doors or within the boundaries of the fenced in backyard. Evan figured they weren't hurting anyone, so there was seldom trouble there.

As was their habit now, Evan and Janie checked in with Donna at the door and then made their way to the bar in the backyard. Evan ordered for them both—Janie drank Cosmopolitans, but Evan either stuck with craft beers or a shot of bourbon over ice. Tonight, he ordered a beer.

"Hey, Janie."

The Jacksons even hired their own bartender for the parties. Evan had no idea where Bronson had come from, but he knew him well enough now to be friendly with him. Not to mention, he figured it might be good to stay on the guy's good side. Evan had never seen Bronson involved in the games, the party activities, but Bronson had probably seen it all and then some. Hell, there had been nights when Evan stood at the bar with Bronson, deep in conversation about cars or the real estate market and watched a lot of things play out at the pool, to the right of the bar.

That had bothered Evan at first. That some people were content to get naked and paw each other right out in the open. But, somehow, he'd gotten used to it. He wasn't sure he liked it—there was something embarrassing about watching other people have sex in real life as opposed to movies—but he sure as hell wouldn't complain about the topless, some-times nude women, who paraded around on nights like these.

"Hey, Bronson." Janie flashed Bronson a big smile as he handed her the bright red drink in a martini glass. "How's it going?"

As always, Evan found himself watching the exchange between his wife and Bronson, wondering if she was attracted to him. If she would fuck him if he was into her. They didn't talk much about the things or people they did once they went home at night. Janie had let him know early on that she'd climaxed more times the first night with a colleague from work than she had in the past year at home. Evan had given her a grim smile and nod and gone down-stairs and punched a hole in the drywall in the storage room in the basement.

He never offered information after the parties, but he was truthful when she asked. Yes, he'd seen the girl with pierced nipples. Yes, the new young blonde was cute, and yes, he'd had a few younger women on their knees in front of him and fuck yes, they were eager to please. But other than that, Evan kept his thoughts to himself.

"Can't complain," Bronson answered with a shrug. Evan grinned as he tipped his bottled beer up for a drink.

"What's the theme tonight?" Janie asked him the same as she did at every party.

"No idea." Bronson's answer was the same as always, too.

"Can't blame a girl for trying," she mumbled. When Evan met Bronson's gaze, the two of them shared a laugh and an eye roll. "You ready?" Janie looked at Evan with big eyes. That excitement could hurt, but she looked at him the same way when they were at home, just the two of them.

"Sure." He nodded, glanced at Bronson with a shrug, and followed his wife into the house where most of the party guests mingled. Sometimes the parties had themes. Planned games—though those were rare. In fact, Evan decided now those nights were special celebrations: wedding showers, special birthdays, retirement parties. Usually, the parties were more laid back. Find a person with blue eyes and see what happens. Or Donna gave everyone their passport and told them to match puzzle pieces or animals or whatever Donna happened to be into at the time.

"Hey."

Evan turned as Frank Jackson approached. He led with an open hand for a shake and merriment in his eyes. The guy was big and wide like a football player. His voice was deep and gruff. But he had the friendliest smile Evan had ever seen, and he appeared to know and like everyone. Evan wasn't into guys, but he had to admit the guy's personality made him pretty attractive.

"Hey, Frank."

Frank pumped his hand. Janie stood at his side, but he heard her excited chatter and figured someone from work had joined them to say hello.

"Didn't see you two sneak in." Frank grinned. "How ya doing?"

"Good." Evan tucked a hand into his hip pocket and took another drink.

"Good to hear it." Frank nodded. He swept his gaze over the growing crowd and then looked around for Donna. Evan knew they attended parties like those they gave, but he wondered when they had time for it. As far as he knew, they rarely took part in the activities at their house, but only because they tended to police things to make sure everyone else was safe.

"Everybody ready?" Donna hollered. When the buzz of conversation didn't stop, Frank whistled for everyone's attention. Evan aimed a grin at Donna; he'd seen her do the same to handle the crowd. She winked at him but turned back to the room at large.

"Evan." Janie tugged at his arm until he removed his hand from his pocket and turned to her. "I want you to meet someone."

He steeled himself. Janie had introduced him to a lot of her coworkers, and he knew a lot of them before he and Janie had become regulars at the Wild Canyon Estates parties. But meeting Janie's friends made him a little apprehensive. He had no desire to shake the hand of any man who might have fucked his wife.

When he turned his head, though, he saw that it was a woman standing beside Janie.

"Kon." Janie brushed her fingers over the woman's bare shoulder, and the woman turned her head. Her green eyes hit him square in the heart and his cock. She looked different, but Evan was staring at Konnor Horton, his star student. The girl's eyes grew wide with interest, but other than that, she didn't react. Not enough for Janie to notice. "Konnor, this is my husband, Evan. Ev, this is Konnor Horton. She's working at the bank now. Donna's her supervisor."

"Hi." Konnor offered her hand; Evan wasn't surprised by her firm shake. The combat boots were gone, as was the faded t-shirt. She wore painted on jeans and dark red sandals with a sexy heel. Her arms were bare, shoulders too, except for the skimpy straps, in the crème-colored tank. Noting the tank straps and nothing else, Evan's eyes roamed over her face—just a touch of makeup, though she had played up her eyes with heavy dark liner and mascara—and down over her shoulders to her breasts.

He was glad for the loose fit of his shorts as he swung his gaze back up to hers.

"Hi, Konnor." When he grinned, Konnor cut loose with a nervous giggle. Janie eyed them curiously.

"Do you know each other?"

"We do." Evan nodded. "Konnor's in my personal finance class."

"Oh my God!"

Maybe it would be nice to see Janie get jealous just once, but on the other hand, Evan decided he might like that free pass tonight. He might make better use of it, so Janie's burst of excitement was a relief.

"Over-achieving star student, blah blah blah." Evan tipped his bottle for a drink and shot Konnor a smirk. She snorted and nodded.

"Right. I think I need a drink." She looked around, probably searching for the bar. "I am so freakin' nervous about being here."

"Don't be nervous." Janie shook her head. "And Evan will get you a drink."

Evan nodded, but Donna hollered again for everyone's attention. He met Konnor's eyes and held up a finger to indicate he would do it in a moment.

"Welcome back," Donna called. "Not much structure tonight. No passports. No pictures to match. No games to play and score. Just one suggested guideline, though it's kind of a help yourself night."

Someone in the back of the room cut loose with an

excited yell. Evan felt the tired grin on his face, though he didn't remember deciding it was funny.

"Try something new," Donna announced.

"That's it?" That voice came from the middle of the room, but Evan couldn't see the woman it belonged to.

"Yep. Mingle. Have a drink. Find someone you're attracted to and see where it leads. But if you're usually into blondes, try a brunette. If you like guys, hang out with a woman. If you like it rough, slow it down."

"Who's gonna know otherwise?"

Donna turned to the left, but again, Evan couldn't see who she answered.

"Nobody." Donna shrugged. "But like I said, it's a help yourself night. Don't let this get stale. Mix it up and do something crazy."

"Um." Konnor's whisper was like fire in his groin. "Like this whole thing isn't crazy."

Evan glanced at her over the top of Janie's head and grinned. "Right?"

"Okay." Donna looked around the circle. "Go have some fun. Just remember. Discretion is key."

Evan felt Konnor's wide eyes on him as Janie turned to him and kissed him.

"Mix it up, Ev." She patted his butt, winked at him, and walked away to find something different. Not better. It was important for Evan to remember that. Janie had promised nothing here was better, just different. And unfortunately for him, his wife needed different now and then.

"Really?"

Evan blinked Konnor into focus and saw that she was staring after Janie, wide-eyed with disbelief.

"Really." He nodded. "C'mon. I'll get you that drink."

3

"So." Evan handed Konnor the longneck bottle and watched her tip it up for a drink. Oblivious to his stare, she swallowed—Evan imagined her shiny, pale lips around his dick—and took a quick peek around the backyard. Safe enough, as things were just getting started. An electronic beat pounded around them, and several couples and groups of people still gathered and talked over their drinks. "You like black coffee and craft beer."

Konnor swung her eyes back around to meet his and grinned as she lowered the bottle.

"I can shoot whiskey, Mr. Bellinger," she assured him. "But I'm not ready for that." She laughed. "I know three people here. No way I wanna be drunk."

"Do not call me Mr. Bellinger here." He tipped his head, but he smiled and arched an eyebrow. "Please."

She chuckled, letting him know she was just messing with him.

"So. Your wife is my friend." She laughed. "Who knew?"

"How long have you worked at the bank?"

"Since March. I was invited to a few other parties, but this is the first time it worked with my schedule."

Evan nodded. "Second job?"

"That, too."

"So, you and Janie? Are you good friends?"

"Well, sure." Konnor nodded. "I mean, I don't work with her often, since I'm on the teller line. But we do lunch sometimes. We do the girls' night at the bar on Wednesdays."

"Okay." He finished his beer and stepped closer to the bar to put the empty bottle down.

"Need another?" Bronson asked him automatically.

"Yes, please."

"You know, I'm stunned that you and Janie are here."

"What do you mean?" He glanced at her as he took the bottle Bronson offered him.

"Well, I know what these kinds of parties are." She wagged her brows at him and laughed softly. "And I know Janie. She's so *married* at work. And you." Konnor tossed her hand up in his direction and shook her head. "Just. Wow."

Evan blinked at her. So much in what Konnor had just said intrigued the hell out of him. He didn't know where to start.

"Wait." He snatched her hand and tugged her a bit closer, thrilled when she stepped into him easily. "What? Me. What? What is that?"

"I mean." She laughed again. Evan sensed her nerves, but not unease. Nerves were understandable. But if he sensed that she was uncomfortable or uneasy about being here or being around him, he would back off. Never mind that there were several other warm, willing women here, Evan wasn't the kind of guy to force himself on any woman. "You're you. You're Mr. Bellinger. You're...a financial analyst."

"And they don't go to parties?" He dragged his eyes over her face, drawn to her lips.

"Well. Not the ones who are married and have kids and talk about their wives and kids in class."

"You know other financial analysts?" he asked with a frown.

"No." She snorted softly. "No, but I've…"

"You've—?"

"I had a fling with one of my professors," she mumbled and shrugged it off. "But no. He wasn't an analyst. He was an econ teacher."

"Here?" Evan squeezed his eyes closed and tried to remember who the econ teacher was at the university.

"No." She shook her head. "No. Back home. Before."

They held the eye contact for a moment, but eventually, Konnor rolled her lips inward and shook her head. "I shouldn't have told you that."

"Why not?"

"I don't know. I feel like you're judging me now."

Evan huffed out a sigh. A woman's high-pitched laugh drew his attention to the pool and reminded him they were standing in the middle of everything, right in front of the bar.

"Wanna walk?"

He held his breath and waited for her to answer. If she said no, he would stand here with her or let her move on to find someone else to talk to.

"Sure." She nodded and linked her fingers with his as they headed back past the temporary bar.

"Who am I to judge you?" he asked as they wandered away from the house. "Look at where we are."

"Yeah, but does a married guy wanna know that he has students who undress him with their eyes and think about him late at night? When they probably shouldn't?"

Evan nearly choked on a mouthful of beer. He thumped his chest and then rubbed it for good measure.

"Yes?"

She laughed softly.

"I like Janie." She tightened her hold on his fingers before he could pull away from her. "She speaks so highly of you. She sounds like the best mom."

"Yeah." Evan flashed her a pained smile. "She's old enough to be your mom. You know that, right? Janie and I are—"

"I'm not as young as you think I am," she promised him.

"How young are you?"

"Twenty-six. With a birthday soon."

"We're old enough to be your parents."

Konnor smiled knowingly and turned to survey the winding pathway through the backyard.

"Does that bother you?" she asked him finally.

"I don't know."

She swung her gaze back to him and dragged her teeth over her lower lip.

"All those thoughts I've had about you." She laughed and rolled her eyes. "And now here we are at an orgy—"

"It's not an—"

"Whatever." Konnor shook her head. "Might as well be."

He couldn't argue with her, because she was right. Instead, he eyed her silently as they walked. There were voices coming from the small alcove where he and Whitney had lingered for most of the last party. Maybe that was for the best. Nothing had happened between them other than a kiss, but it might feel weird to hang out with someone else in the same spot.

"So." Konnor cleared her throat. Fingers still linked with his, she rubbed her thumb over his skin. "This is okay with you?"

Evan narrowed his eyes at her when she glanced at him.

"Define *this*."

"Your wife hooking up with other guys? That doesn't bother you?"

"What do you think, Konnor?" He shrugged his lips and then tipped his bottle up for a drink.

"Then why do you do it?"

He started to answer, but she shook her head. "Sorry. First rule is discretion. Second is keep it impersonal, right?"

"If you haven't been to Donna and Frank's house, how do you know about these parties?" Evan was genuinely curious about Konnor, but he also wondered if someone was talking about their experiences at Wild Canyon Estates.

"I've been to other parties like this," she mumbled. "Pretty hard to misunderstand Donna's announcement, right?"

He grinned when she cut her eyes to him and then looked away.

"Janie likes the parties," he told her, deciding for now to keep his explanation simple. She wasn't searching for reassurance or trying to figure out how to handle this sort of infidelity the way Whitney had been at the last party. Konnor was sincerely curious about him and Janie, but he sensed it was something entirely different. She was flirting with him. "I'll do whatever I can to make her happy."

"Yeah?" They stopped walking near the fence at the back of the yard. It was still daylight, though the sun had dropped a bit in the western sky. Still plenty of light to see the blue shine in her hair; Evan wanted to run his fingers through it to see if it was as silky as it looked. "And what about you? Do you get involved, or do you pass the time away talking to the bartender?"

"Depends." He shrugged one shoulder.

"Wow." Konnor hitched a deep breath and then blew it out with a nervous laugh.

"Tell me about your econ professor."

"Eww." She shook her head. "Do I have to? That was an epic fuck up on my part."

"Why?"

"He was just sort of a dick," she answered. She took the last few steps to stand by the fence. Evan watched her duck her chin to her chest and cursed the weak sunlight that touched her hair. She was gorgeous in this light. Maybe she knew he was watching her closely, but she didn't look at him when she lifted her head and drank from the bottle. Evan had a sudden desire to kiss her. Sure, he'd imagined her lips around his cock at least a hundred times by now, but he wanted to *kiss* her. A slow, wet kiss on her mouth, her lithe body pressed up against his.

Sunlight meant the neighbors behind the house could see them clearly if they happened to be at home. Didn't matter, since his wife was at the same party, but still. Donna and Frank had sex parties, but they were still classy, and Evan didn't plan to be the person to put on a show for the neighbors.

"Did he hurt you?" Evan moved to stand beside her.

"No." She met his eyes. "Not like that. But he was very controlling."

"Why were you in an econ class before now?"

Konnor arched her eyebrow and offered him a tiny smile.

"Lots of reasons, Evan."

"How old were you when this happened?"

"Twenty-one." She stared at him boldly. "Don't stand there and feel bad for me. He didn't take anything I didn't willingly give him. And when I had enough, I called it off."

Evan stared at her silently, but she held the eye contact without flinching.

"Okay." He reached for her hand again.

"Where are we going?" She held her ground, resisting when he tried to pull her back to the path to the house.

"Back that way."

"Why?" She nibbled on her lower lip. "I thought…"

"It's not dark yet," he said simply. "I have no idea which of Donna and Frank's neighbors know what goes on here."

"Gotcha." She nodded and walked with him again. "How long have you guys been doing this?"

"Married twenty-seven years," he looked over at her as they walked, "and we've been doing the parties for about a year, I guess."

"And your kids? Do they—"

"God, no." Evan shook his head.

He was surprised to see the deep end of the pool empty as they approached the house. It crossed his mind to suggest sitting on the side, but he closed his mouth when he remembered she had jeans on. Hell yes, he wanted her out of her pants, but the fact that she was his student still made him hesitant.

"Need another beer?" he offered.

"Please."

"Still not ready for the hard stuff?"

Her throaty laugh stroked his balls and made his dick so hard it hurt. She gave him an embarrassed grin—fuck, if that blush on her cheeks didn't make his dick damned near explode—and folded her arms over her chest.

"Um." She rubbed her fingers over her lips and tipped her head at him. "I am. Yes. If you're bringing it, I'm ready."

Evan laughed, but she licked her lips in what appeared to be a nervous gesture rather than a shot at seduction. He needed a distraction. Something boring like numbers so he could talk his dick down.

"But no whiskey," she said quietly. "Not yet."

"I'll be right back."

He felt her eyes on his back as he walked the length of the pool and approached the bar. Bronson hit him with two longnecks, shot a quick look over at Konnor, and then gave Evan a subtle nod. The sunset hung low and lazy when he turned back to Konnor. Pale pastels lined the darkening sky. The party lights strung throughout the trees in Donna and Frank's yard glowed, though they still competed with the lingering daylight.

"Is this okay?" Konnor nodded at the pool when Evan handed her a bottle. "Sitting out here for a while?"

"Sure." He watched her take a long pull from the bottle and then lean over to set it on the ground by the pool. The club music still pounded around them, which at least made most conversations hard to hear. Still, Evan would have preferred to find a private place to do whatever it was they were going to do. He kicked out of his flip-flops and watched her do the same. Her right foot caught in her shoe, though, and she hopped for a second on one foot. Evan's eyes were drawn to her breasts, loose in the tank.

"Damn." She laughed and reached for him to steady herself as she tugged the sandal off. Evan's skin was on fire where her fingers were wrapped around his wrist.

"You okay?" He grinned when she put her foot down and looked up at him.

"Got it." She let go of his wrist, and Evan almost reached for her hand. No, they weren't just going to stand here for the duration of the night with her holding on to his hand. But that skin on skin contact was delicious, and he wanted more of it. She flashed him a small smile as her hands went to the button of her jeans. Evan muttered a streak of expletives, because for the first time in a long time, he was worried about controlling himself. He wanted those lips around his cock, fuck yes. But he also wanted to drive his cock balls deep inside her and see her head thrown back in ecstasy. What if he shot his wad the second he sank into her pussy?

Her fingers deftly unbuttoned her jeans. Evan dragged his eyes up from her hands to meet her gaze. She stared at him for a moment, but Evan dropped his gaze to watch when she eased her zipper down and parted the denim.

"Fuck." He groaned at the stretch of smooth, tan skin and the low waistband of what appeared to be tiny bikini panties.

"Is this okay?" This time her words were just a whisper. Evan nodded as his eyes made that long, slow climb from her open jeans to her eyes. She stared at him silently, and for just a second, Evan saw his student, Konnor Horton, rather than the sexy-as-fuck girl his wife had introduced him to earlier.

"Perfect." He shoved the worry down and nodded again.

They could have been alone on a deserted island. They could have been center stage in a packed arena. Evan had eyes only for Konnor as she pushed her jeans down and stepped out of them. Mouth dry, he watched her fold them up and lean over to set them on her sandals. *Fucked.* His hungry eyes devoured her naked ass cheeks—just as perfect as he'd imagined the other day—and the tiny strip of pink lace between them.

"Do you wear that in my class?"

She straightened and stepped closer to the pool. "The thong? God, no."

He watched her as she lowered herself gracefully to sit poolside.

"Are you gonna sit down?" She looked up at him expectantly.

He sat, though probably not with her grace or seductive prowess. Then again, she was watching him with a very intense gaze, so she saw something in him that she liked.

"I hate thongs," she told him when they were sitting side by side. "I'd rather just go commando."

"Also sexy as fuck," he mumbled. "But that little flash of pink just about gave me a fucking heart attack."

She laughed softly. "What if I wear it to your class some-times and you just have to look at me and guess if I'm wearing it or not?"

"Cruel."

"Or I could just go commando and let you think about that during class." She turned her head to look at him, teeth tugging at her lower lip.

"You're a hellcat. You know that, right?"

The blush tinged her cheeks again, but she looked away quickly. Evan found the alternating shy and seductive woman intriguing. His dick was a steel rod tucked painfully in his shorts, and he was desperate to get his hands on her.

On the other hand, he didn't want to rush it. This. The night. What would Janie say if she knew he'd finally found someone he wanted to lie down with and fuck the daylights out of? Long and hard and slow.

The thought made him hurt. Again. Konnor glanced at him when he adjusted his dick in his shorts.

"She's not gonna walk out here and see us together and get pissed, right?"

"Janie?" He coughed. "Konnor, she's probably flat on her back with a guy between her legs right now."

Konnor flinched.

"I'm not trying to be harsh. This is just who she is right now."

"And you? Do you have limits?"

Evan started to answer her, but he hesitated.

"It's okay." She shrugged. "I do, too."

"Okay." He nodded. "Yeah, I suppose I do. But I don't know what they are."

She eyed him carefully.

"Does that make sense?"

"I get it," she answered quietly. "But I'm asking if you're usually fucking someone else by now, too."

"No." He shook his head.

Konnor drew in a deep breath.

"Konnor?"

Chin tipped down, she looked at him through her lashes. A shy smile played at her lips.

"I have been to parties like this, and I have done…things. But…"

"But what?" he urged her.

"With strangers. With guys I sort of know. With my step-brothers' friends. But not like this."

Evan's dick wept at her uncertainty. He wanted to strip this girl bare and lick her from head to toe. He wanted to slide his fingers between her legs and fuck her with his tongue and then climb inside her and ride her until he died and went to heaven.

But he wouldn't force a thing on her.

"What do you mean *like this*?" He gave her a gentle nudge with his elbow.

"I told you I think about you at night," she whispered.

A little thrill kicked up his spine and woke his dick up again. Still, he had to be sure. He wasn't the guy to keep plying a skittish girl with alcohol until she gave in. He wasn't sure anyone here would do such a thing. Frank and Donna were good judges of character, and everyone here seemed to be on board with participating or okay with staying a spectator.

"Konnor." Evan reached for her, curled his fingers around her chin, and tilted her head up to look at him. "Do you want to do this? Because it's okay—"

"I have wanted to do…things with you since the first day of class," she admitted. "I was watching you, undressing you with my eyes, and then you called on me to ask me something about savings accounts versus IRAs, and I thought I was gonna die of embarrassment. I thought you could tell what I was thinking."

"Nope." He rubbed his thumb over her lips.

"I just don't want this to be weird next week."

Evan had no doubt that it would be different next week if he fucked her tonight. But that didn't mean it would have to be weird, did it?

"We don't have to—"

"Don't say that," she argued and covered his hand with hers. "Don't say we don't have to do this. Evan, I want to do this."

Her words took his breath away. Rather than speak, he leaned in to kiss her. With just the slightest touch of his lips on hers, his heartrate spiked, and his blood shot straight to his groin.

"I was gonna say we don't have to let it get weird."

His mouth still close enough to hers to touch, he felt the soft, warm little puff of laughter that escaped her lips. She nodded, her hand still covering his, and tilted her head to the side to study him. Evan dragged his eyes over her face to her mouth and kissed her again. Her lips were warm and soft, and she kissed him back but still let him control the moment.

He angled his body toward hers and traced a path up her arm with his free hand.

"Can I tell you something?" she whispered the words over his lips, though no one could hear them over the music.

"What?"

"I don't do much kissing," she admitted. "Feels too…" She shrugged.

"Do you want me to stop kissing you?"

She moved her hand now and stroked her fingers over his jaw. "No. I really want you to kiss me again."

4

Desire made his heart pound, and his dick thick and long, and damned if one night with her would ever be enough. Evan pressed his thumb to her lip and sucked in a quick breath when she flicked it with the tip of her tongue. Hungry to touch all of her, to smooth his hands over her warm, soft skin, to mold her breasts in his hands, he reminded himself that it might be one night, but there was no hurry. The parties lasted until the last guest went home, no matter the time, and tonight had just started.

Still, he wanted more. Now.

He wanted to know what the skin behind her ear tasted like. He wanted to nip at her collar bone and then lick a trail to her perfectly sculpted shoulders. He wanted to drag his teeth over her nipples, and he wanted to press his open mouth to the inside of her wrists and flick his tongue over the back of her knees.

He wanted to hear her voice, thick with desire, say his name as he moved inside her.

He wanted to know why she went to parties like this but

didn't do much kissing, and he wanted to know what exactly she thought about him at night when she was in her bed.

Evan slid his hand over her shoulder and then combed his fingers up through her hair. Konnor rewarded him with a moan of pleasure. Intrigued by what she'd said, even more intrigued by what she hadn't said, and enthralled by the mysteries of her body, he lowered his lips to hers again for another gentle, curious kiss.

The mix of passionate woman and wide-eyed girl in his arms made him ultra-aware of the moment. His first kisses with Janie were so long ago now; he remembered them, of course. He remembered the first date and the kiss goodnight, but the memories were comfortable and worn. Making love to Janie *now* was new, after all the encounters she'd had here at the parties, and though it had been hard for him to swallow the new normal, he got it now.

He loved his wife. He loved taking her to bed, whether it was to linger there all morning and make love or to fuck hard and fast in ten free minutes. He loved watching their sons play ball, and he loved taking an evening walk with her after dinner. Holding her hand and listening to her voice as she told him about her day.

But he wanted the woman in his arms. He wanted every piece of Konnor Horton, body and soul.

And what he felt for her had absolutely nothing to do with his wife.

That had been what bothered him about Janie needing other men to deliver her to orgasm. As much as he loved her and wanted her to find that pleasure—even if it meant other lovers—he hadn't understood how she could still want to be with him.

He found the answer in the hooded emerald eyes looking back at him now. This beautiful girl in his arms was all that mattered in this moment, but he knew he would leave the party with his wife, and he knew that they would shower together—just a shower after a party like this —and find each other again in the morning. Tomorrow when he made love to Janie, he wouldn't think about Konnor, but right now, he wanted to concentrate on this, here and now.

"I love the taste of beer on your lips," he told her. A low, growly laugh rumbled up from her belly. He smiled, mouth over hers, and swallowed her laugh. "I bet whiskey would taste even better."

"It might," she agreed, "but no."

"You know I have a hundred questions." He dropped staccato kisses over her cheek to her ear and then tugged the lobe with his teeth. She shivered dramatically and dropped her chin to her chest.

"About me?"

"Mm-hmm." He flicked his tongue up the shell of her ear, feeling the hardware there and wondering what it felt like for her when he licked her. He nibbled at her neck, his fingers still sliding through her hair.

"You're not supposed to ask questions," she reminded him.

"You don't want to answer them." He moved his hand to cup the back of her neck and then smooth over her back. Konnor eased into him and rested her forehead on his shoulder.

"I'd rather not." Her words were gruff and strangled, as if she had tried to trap them in her throat. Evan didn't want to let it go; he wanted to know who Konnor was before she'd just shown up in his classroom, and he wanted to know more about the parties she'd been to—the ones that made her blush to talk about, and he wanted to know why she didn't do much kissing.

She inched closer to him. Evan moaned when he felt her

teeth on his neck. She wrapped her hand around his shoulder and lapped at his skin with her tongue.

"Evan." She licked a trail to his lips again and then met his gaze. "I can't do this here."

He blinked. He couldn't do it anywhere else. Somehow the party atmosphere made it okay. Moving something like this away from the party, away from Janie, felt like cheating.

"I mean the pool."

He watched her sink her teeth into her lip and stare at him with wide eyes. Without a word, he untangled himself from her hold and climbed to his feet. Konnor took his hand when he offered it to help her up. Evan grabbed both bottles as she leaned over to scoop up her jeans and slide them on. She had to tug a bit as her legs were wet from the pool, and Evan's heart melted a little when she peeked at him and laughed softly. She simply carried her shoes as they walked away from the pool. He might feel a little weird about parading into the house to find a room where they could play, but no one was watching them. Not even Bronson.

Besides, how many nights had he waited Janie out? He had given in to his base desires, and he would never complain about the times he'd had women on their knees in front of him with their mouths on his dick. But this was something entirely different, this blinding lust he felt for the girl he led hand in hand back to the house and down the hall to the first open doorway.

He hadn't done this before. He hadn't gone looking for a bedroom, let alone leading a girl he desperately wanted to fuck to a bedroom where they could be alone. They slipped inside with quiet whispers about where they were, what the room might be. Evan didn't care if it was a bathroom or an office; if he could close the door, it was a perfect.

Once inside, back pressed against the closed door, he looked around the dark room. Only a tiny bit of dark orange fell through the gap in the drapes on the far wall, but as his eyes adjusted to the dim room, he could make out a loveseat and a big screen TV. It was a small room, apparently a den, but there was no clutter to make it appear lived in.

Evan looked down when he heard the muted clunk of Konnor's sandals on the carpeted floor. Jeans still unbuttoned at her waist, she reached for the bottles he carried. Evan's gaze trailed after her as she crossed the room to put them on an end table by the loveseat. Denim covered her now, but his dick summoned up the image of her bare ass out by the pool. His heart rate sky-rocketed, but he felt a flash of guilt. He'd never been unfaithful to Janie. She didn't count a blowjob as cheating; in fact, she had been pushing him from the first party to do more and explore his boundaries. She wouldn't even consider this, fucking Konnor, cheating, because this was the new normal in their marriage.

Konnor turned to him, but she hesitated when she saw that he hadn't moved from his spot at the door. Eyes locked with hers, he watched as Konnor took a few steps toward him, and he moved—led by his dick—and there she was. Her long, lithe body pressed against him. Her hands slid haltingly up over his arms, and the patch of bare skin on her stomach pressed against his middle as she looped her arms loosely around his neck.

Evan clamped his hands on her hips and yanked that spot of bare skin hard against him. He shuddered at the press of her tight belly on his dick. With her arms around his neck, the flowery scent of her perfume surrounded him, and thoughts, worries about Janie melted away.

His hands moved without communication from his brain. One second, they rested on her hips, and the next, they were inside her jeans, his fingers cupping the smooth, soft skin of her ass. Konnor feathered her fingers in his business-length haircut, making him wish he had the longer, unruly curls from the old days when he and Janie first met.

She tipped her head back to look at him and parted her lips in invitation. Evan fought the urge to devour her, to catch her tongue in his mouth and take her lips and swallow her whole. His greedy dick throbbed in encouragement, and his body vibrated with need, but he pressed his lips to hers again in that slow, controlled curious kiss.

He had a free pass to fuck around, but that didn't mean he had to rush a damned thing.

"Are you always this gentle?" Her voice was drowsy and thick when he trailed his lips from hers over her cheek and then nipped at her neck.

"Am I boring you?" he whispered his words over her neck and then rubbed them in with the tip of his tongue. Her low, knowing laughter lit a fire in his blood.

"No." In the waning daylight, Evan saw the flicker of desire in her eyes. "I'm not sure you could bore me. But I'm not fragile, Evan."

"We have all night." He smoothed his thumb over her lips again, sucking in a sharp breath when Konnor scraped her teeth over the pad. "And I like the marathon approach, Konnor. Long and slow and steady."

Something like fear flickered in her eyes, but Evan couldn't be sure, because she closed them and lowered her chin again. Before he could ask, before he could make sure she was okay, she licked his thumb, still on her lips, and then sucked him into her mouth. Her lips tugged at his thumb sending a jolt of electricity straight to his dick.

"God, you're beautiful." He clamped his teeth together as she moved in his arms. Her hands were gone from his hair, but she smoothed them down over his shoulders and then tugged at the tail of his shirt. Untucked, it slid up easily, and then Konnor's hot, hungry hands were on his skin.

She pushed his shirt up over his stomach and his chest, her hands molding his body and her fingertips flicking his nipples. Her eyes shot up to his when the flat brown discs grew hard under her touch.

"Don't tell me I'm beautiful." She shook her head.

He wanted to argue, to ask her why she wouldn't want those words. But she moved again before he could voice his concern. She stepped back, leaving his middle where she'd been pressed against him cold. Hungry for her touch, he watched her hands gather the tail of her tank top. She pulled it up and over her head. From the corner of his eye, he saw her drop it to the floor, but he kept his gaze on her bare breasts, perfectly round and proud.

"Did Janie tell you? Before tonight?"

"Tell me what?" Her thick, buttery voice made him hot and achy.

"What to expect?" He shrugged. "Or is this your everyday party outfit?"

When she didn't answer him, he dragged his eyes from her breasts—he had yet to touch her—and looked up to meet her gaze.

"Am I boring you, Evan?" She looked amused, a tiny smile on her lips.

"There's no way in hell you could bore me," he said simply.

"Then touch me." She raised her eyebrows expectantly, hopefully maybe. Evan stepped closer again, regretting now that they'd found a den, rather than a bedroom. He ached to strip Konnor down and lay her out before him to spread her legs and taste her.

She sighed with content when he touched her. He cupped her breasts in his hands, reveling in the weight of them in his palms. Konnor arched her back and moaned softly when he rolled her nipples with his thumbs. Determined to take her slowly, to appreciate every inch of her skin, Evan grabbed her hand when she moved to touch him again.

"I don't do slow, Evan." She pressed her lips to his to cut off any arguments. Her hands were at the tail of his shirt again, shoving it out of her way. Done fighting her, Evan let go of her hand and tugged his shirt over his head. Konnor's fingers deftly worked the button and zipper of his shorts as he dropped his shirt somewhere near hers. He stepped out of his flip-flops as she pushed his shorts down over his hips so he could kick out of them.

In his snug briefs now, his cock straining to be closer to her, to get inside her, Evan watched her shimmy out of her jeans. Finally, standing before him in the skimpy pink thong, Konnor held her head high and stared at him boldly.

"I wanna fuck you blind, Konnor." His low, gravelly voice cut through the thick, electric tension in the room. He let his eyes roam over her body as she shivered with anticipation. He reached for his shorts at his feet to retrieve a condom from his wallet, but Konnor stepped closer to him and stroked his cock through his briefs.

Their eyes met again, and then she slid her fingers under the waistband of his briefs and tugged them down. Her long, elegant fingers wrapped around his shaft, and she smoothed her thumb over his head.

"Wait." She held the eye contact as she lowered herself to her knees in front of him. Evan struggled to get naked as she licked fire from his balls to the tip of his cock.

"Jesus, Konnor." He arched his back and thrust into her immediately.

"This is what I think about at night." Her whisper carried over his thighs and his cock and up over his stomach. "What you taste like. Licking your cock and taking you in my mouth and making you come."

Knees weak, he took a few steps backwards until he

felt the wall at his back. Konnor moved easily with him. Her fingertips skated up the backs of his thighs as she flicked his balls gently with the tip of her tongue. When she sank her fingers hard into his ass, Evan tangled his fingers in her soft hair and pressed her harder to his cock.

"Do you like this?" Her open mouth pressed to his balls, her words vibrated against him and made him gasp out loud with pleasure. "Have you ever thought about me sucking you off, Evan?"

"Yes."

Why lie? There was no turning back from where they were right now.

"Do you think about fucking me?" She still spoke against his balls, but now she stroked his cock with the flat of her tongue, licking in long, powerful strokes until she reached the top and closed her lips around his head.

"I wanna bury my face between your legs, Konnor," he said through gritted teeth. She sucked him hard for a moment and then eased the pressure long enough to lick him again, careful to let the tip of her tongue play at the tiny slit in the head of his cock. "Careful."

"Come, Evan." She teased him again with quick flicks of her tongue, and then she sucked him again, her head bobbing as she moved him in and out of her mouth. With the head of his cock at the back of her throat and one hand massaging his balls, Evan lost control when she squeezed his ass cheek with her free hand.

Fingers fisted in her hair, he cut loose a low shout and a grunt as he erupted in her mouth. Konnor, unfazed, continued to milk the orgasm from him, swallowing his release. The door opened, but Evan was too far gone to care. Konnor didn't appear to notice.

"Mind if I join you guys?"

Janie slipped inside and pushed the door closed behind her.

The last of the late orange sunlight had faded, leaving the room in grim shades of gray, but Evan could see that Janie was relaxed, as if she'd already ridden someone to orgasm tonight. She sipped from her drink and offered him an elated smile as she crossed the room to set it down near his and Konnor's bottles.

Konnor drew away from him, but she appeared unaffected by Janie's sudden appearance. Rather than rush to get away from him, she licked his now flaccid cock again before slowly climbing to her feet in front of him.

"Do you still wanna fuck me?" she whispered, a tiny lift in her brow.

To answer her question, he reached again for his shorts to get a condom from his wallet. He was a bit rattled to find his knees were still weak, and Konnor was watching him with hooded eyes, licking her lips like she wanted more, and his wife was watching them with lust in her eyes.

"Janie." His voice was gruff.

"I've seen that look on your face." She tipped one corner of her mouth up in a smile. "I'm gonna assume Konnor knows what she's doing."

Evan reached for his wife and leaned in to kiss her when she moved toward him.

"Can I watch?" she whispered.

He hadn't known watching was a turn-on for his wife, but he wasn't sure why it surprised him.

"You don't wanna play, too?" Konnor turned to Janie with wide eyes. Evan hadn't thought it possible, but his cock stirred and then throbbed with need when the two women shared a kiss. The ease of the kiss almost suggested it wasn't their first, but Konnor hadn't come to a party before, so she hadn't kissed *his wife* before now.

"Are you okay with that?" Janie ended the kiss.

"Mmm." Konnor nodded. "Not my first rodeo."

"Ev?"

He wasn't about to admit it was, indeed, his first rodeo with two women at the same time. Janie had to know it; they'd been together forever, and they'd learned the finer points of sex together when they were kids. She also had to know that he hadn't fucked anyone at a Wild Canyon Estates party. But he didn't have to say it out loud.

His cock stretched thick and long, and Konnor's nipples were hard and begging for his mouth. He had no intention of drawing out conversation.

5

Janie slipped out of her dress with ease that would have bothered him at any other time. Tonight, Evan simply watched her and marveled at the fact that he had two beautiful women ready to play. He watched in stunned silence as Janie moved closer to Konnor and hooked her fingers in her panties. Konnor reached for Janie, sliding her fingers up her stomach to cup her breast. Evan's blood burned with desperation as his wife gasped softly, first with surprise and then with pleasure. He watched them kiss again, his eyes drawn to the slide of Konnor's tongue over Janie's lips.

He wanted to slide his tongue over their skin, over Janie's breasts and Konnor's thighs. Konnor, still kissing his wife, reached blindly for him. Without hesitation, Evan moved to stand behind her and rested his hands on her hips. She grinded against him, twerking her naked ass against his cock.

"Fuck her, Ev." Janie looked at him over Konnor's shoulder. "I want to watch."

Janie snatched his wallet up from his shorts, where he'd abandoned it yet again. Her eyes devoured every move his hands made as he sculpted Konnor's hips and breasts, his fingertips hungry for the feel of her hard nipples.

He and Konnor watched Janie tear open the condom wrapper with her teeth, but Konnor stepped away from him so Janie could roll the condom over his cock. Evan watched Janie's fingers on his shaft, but his eyelids slid closed when she cradled his balls in her hand for a moment.

Again, he wished they had more room, but when Konnor leaned into the loveseat, Evan zeroed in on her sweet little ass. He wanted her breasts in his face, the taste of her arousal on his tongue, but his cock was straining desperately to get inside her. She peeked at him over her shoulder, her lips curved up in a grin.

Evan grabbed her ass and spread her open. Heart pounding in his throat and his fingers and mostly in his cock, he stepped up behind her and drove into her hard and deep. Her tight, wet heat engulfed him. He nipped at her shoulder, but he held himself still for just a moment.

"Fuck me, Evan." She wiggled against him.

Janie hovered behind him as he eased out of Konnor and then drove her hard and deep again.

"Have you watched two people do this, Evan? It makes me wanna touch myself." Janie's breath was hot on his shoulder. He gasped when she pressed against him, her breasts soft and warm on his back. Konnor moaned softly as he continued to move behind her, sliding in and out of her heat. He wanted to touch her, to slide his hand around her hips and slip his fingers between her legs to touch her clit. Evan wanted to drive Konnor out of her mind, but he felt her squeezing him, urging him to go faster, making him lose control. With the press of his wife's body at his back and her hands molding his chest and his thighs, he gave in to the pleasure and rode Konnor hard and fast.

When the orgasm tore through him, Janie's hands cupped

his inner thighs and squeezed, while Konnor continued to milk him, squeezing him hard inside her body. She straightened and reached for his hands, placing them over her breasts. Evan nipped at her shoulder and her neck, hands roaming with greed when she turned in his arms.

She kissed him with the same mouth she'd kissed his wife, the same tongue that had licked his cock only minutes before. Evan painted his hands low over Konnor's belly and finally moved his fingers over what had to be a sexy-as-fuck Brazilian—the daylight had drained from the sky so he couldn't see her clearly now—and flicked her clit.

"Janie's turn," she whispered into his mouth. "My turn to watch."

Janie's hands were on him again, and Konnor stood behind him, grazing her teeth over his shoulders, chasing a thrill up his spine. Janie took the condom from his limp dick and dropped it in her nearly empty glass.

They'd been coming to the Wild Canyon Estates parties for a year, but they had never come here and messed around together. Touching his wife's breasts had never been such a thrill as now, and Evan knew it was as much because Konnor was watching as the fact that they were guests at a party where anything goes. Forgetting that Janie might have already been with someone tonight—he had always needed a night between them before he could make love to her after a party—he reached for her, hungry to take what she offered.

Janie moved, backed up against the wall where she'd originally found him with Konnor on her knees before him. Evan's cock throbbed and stretched, but he had time to pleasure her first. Janie's eyes grew big with excitement when she read his intention in his eyes. He felt Konnor's gaze as he lowered his head to suck Janie's nipple into his mouth.

Konnor pressed into him and wound her arms around him. Evan's heartbeat hammered when her fingers circled his shaft again and gave a gentle tug. He turned his attention to Janie's other breast, rubbed his lips over the heavy curve and then flicked his tongue over her nipple. Konnor stroked him again and eased in to kiss Janie when he moved to his knees in front of her.

His cock throbbed now, hungry for his wife's familiar wet heat. Janie spread her legs for him and smoothed her fingers over his hair as he dipped his head and licked her clit. Next time, he would stake the house out early and find a bed where the three of them could slide over each other's bodies. Janie moaned softly when he opened her with his thumbs and licked her again, pressing his tongue up into her wet folds. The thought of plunging his tongue inside Konnor the same way shot a powerful pain down through his gut and his dick.

"Fuck me, Ev," Janie whispered.

He wanted to stand and drive his cock into his wife and pound her against the wall. She would wind her legs around his waist and meet him thrust for thrust, and all too quickly, it would be over. First, he wanted to make her sob his name with pleasure.

Konnor's hands were in his hair now, and her lips were on Janie's neck. Evan thrust two fingers inside Janie and curled them to rub the spot that made her buck with pleasure and pain. Satisfaction gripped him and pumped through him when she moaned loud and long, his name spilling from her lips. The parties, sex with other men, had been an open playground for her to let loose and find the things she liked. Evan thanked his lucky stars she had shared those spots with him and asked him to touch her the way she learned she liked.

He scissored his fingers inside her again and tugged her clit into his mouth, sucking the engorged, sensitive skin. Janie came hard, the walls of her sex clenching tight around his fingers. Evan drew the orgasm out for her, sliding his fingers over her G-spot again and again, until she sobbed and chanted his name.

When she stopped quivering, he stood and rubbed his way up her body. Cock hard and ready, he probed at her folds and sighed with pleasure when she lifted her legs to wrap them around his hips and took him in. Fucking Konnor had been incredible and fast and outrageous, because he'd been with Janie for the past twenty-seven years. Fucking Janie—bareback—was like a backyard band playing folk music. Perfectly comfortable and everything he would always need and come home to.

Tonight, it was more. The air around them was charged with tension, the smell of sex. Konnor was still at his back, her hands sliding over his hips.

"I can't do it again," Janie whispered, and Evan might have been swept back into the times before when Janie couldn't orgasm, except that she'd just come apart under his mouth. Still, he hated that they were fucking against a wall, in the dark, and he couldn't find an angle to make it work for her. "Ev, it's okay."

"I want this to be good for you, J." He kissed her cheek and then pressed a sloppy, open-mouthed kiss on the corner of her lips.

"Janie." Konnor kissed his shoulder. Evan felt his heartrate go insane when Konnor reached between him and Janie. His own breathing grew ragged, but when Konnor rubbed her finger over Janie's clit and his wife yelped with pleasure, he drew back to stare at Janie in the darkness.

"Okay?" he asked quietly. In the near darkness, their eyes met. He couldn't see her well, but his eyes focused on her teeth as they scraped over her lip. "What? Tell me."

"Is it? Okay?" she whispered.

"Whatever you need, J," he promised her.

She nodded. Evan wasn't sure if Konnor saw her, but she had to have heard their exchange.

"Janie?"

His wife's name ghosted over his skin in another woman's voice.

"Yes."

Janie writhed against the wall as Evan slowly pumped his hips against hers and Konnor moved her fingers between their bodies, over Janie's sensitive skin. His wife burst just a moment later, his name on her lips, and then as she dipped her forehead to rest on Evan's shoulder, she whispered Konnor's name in wonder. Evan held her as he pressed harder and faster toward his own orgasm.

Janie tightened her legs around his waist when his body went tight and stiff with his release. Heartbeat roaring in his ears now, his heart thudding wildly in his chest, Evan kissed Janie's hair and her cheek and her neck, and then rested his cheek on hers as they drifted back to earth, to their sweaty, satiated bodies, both of them too weak to move.

"Wow." Janie finally let her legs slide down over his until she stood before him. "That was different."

Evan wished he could see her face better in the darkness. Different how? Good? Bad? Because they'd never been together at a Wild Canyon Estates party? Or because Janie hadn't participated in a threesome? Or because Konnor was with them?

"Konnor?" Evan's voice was gritty with satisfaction and exhaustion.

"Mmm." Janie mistook his uttering Konnor's name as a question to her. Was what had happened between them different because of Konnor? When Konnor didn't answer him, he stepped back from his wife, dragged his hands down over her sides and her bare hips, and finally turned to check on Konnor.

"Konnor?" he said again. She was gone.

"Where'd she go?" Janie sounded as surprised as he felt.

Evan scrubbed his hands over his face and then moved back to the door, looking for a light switch. He slid his hand along the wall and muttered in frustration when he found nothing but smooth wall.

"Did you hear the door?" he asked Janie.

"No." Janie stepped away from the door. In the shadows of the room, he watched her snag her dress from the floor and turn it right side out. "But then, I was kind of preoccupied."

Even in the cover of the darkness, Evan saw Janie flash him a soft, sweet smile.

"Maybe we should do this more often," he suggested. Janie's eyes followed his movements as he pulled his briefs and then shorts up over his hips.

"Add a third person to the mix? Or invite Konnor Horton?"

"Well, I meant you and me making love here at the parties, but…" He shrugged and let his words trail off.

"Do you think she's okay?" Janie looked around again. Evan stared at her silently when she stepped around him and turned on the lamp. Their eyes met, and yes, he was concerned about Konnor, but for just a second, he couldn't breathe. Janie knew her way around here. Had she been with someone else in this room at a party in the past? Had someone bent her backwards over the couch? Or had she sucked someone off the way Konnor had pleasured him?

Overwhelmed with rage at the thought, he turned his back to Janie and hung his head.

"Ev?"

"Gimme a minute, Janie," he mumbled. He took a deep breath, nostrils flared wide, and counted to three.

"What's wrong?"

"Nothing." He shook his head and bent at the waist to grab his shirt from the floor. Konnor's was nowhere to be found.

"Her clothes are gone." Janie sounded concerned.

Evan pulled his shirt on and then rubbed his eyes vigorously. He didn't like it, either, but there wasn't much they could do about it at the moment.

"She only drank two beers," he told Janie. "She should be fine to drive."

"Yeah, but," Janie argued. "I mean. Do you think she's okay?"

"I don't know." He sighed, thoughts on the mix of femme fatale and innocence in the girl who had snuck out of the room unnoticed. "She mentioned that she'd been to parties like this. And she didn't seem...uncomfortable."

Janie laughed softly. "I guess I just wish she hadn't rushed off like that."

"Me, too," he agreed.

In fact, the worry over her soured his stomach. It wasn't his first concern, but Konnor was his student, and they'd sure as hell crossed the line a hundred times over tonight. He wasn't worried that she would point her finger and accuse him of sexual misconduct or assault. But he was worried that they'd fucked things up and made it weird.

He was still curious as hell by all the things she hadn't said, too, but he didn't want to stand here in Frank and Donna Jackson's den surrounded by empty drinks, a used condom, and the smell of sex lingering in the air.

"Let's go home, J." He shot Janie a hopeful peek, afraid that she wasn't ready to leave. That she would want or need something new, more. She slipped her fingers in his hand and nodded, her smile almost enough to erase his misgivings about what had just happened.

6

Evan was happy the rest of the weekend rolled by without incident, but he wanted to grab it with both hands and yank it by faster. He and Janie dug into the garage and cleaned it out Saturday. It was a pain in the ass, amazing to him that so much junk could accumulate so quickly—didn't seem that long ago that they'd cleaned it out last—but on the other hand, it kept his mind off Konnor Horton.

Sort of.

It felt weird to worry about her when he was at home with his wife and kids, so he didn't mention it. He didn't say her name, didn't bring up the wild things they'd done in that little room in the Jacksons' house. But Janie did. Evan tried to hide his relief that Janie said Konnor's name first, but by saying her name, she made it okay for him to talk about her, too. The way Janie's eyes had watched him intently when they wondered if Konnor was okay told him that she knew he had been thinking about her.

On Sunday, he worked in the yard and scrubbed the deck with the power washer. While it was all stuff that needed to be done, Evan was desperate to keep his mind off Konnor.

He reminded himself as he trimmed the evergreen bushes behind the house that she was an adult, and she had walked into Friday night with her eyes wide open.

Didn't help.

By Monday morning, when Evan stood at the podium in his finance classroom, he was completely caught up in the girl who didn't do slow but also didn't do much kissing. He wondered what Janie would think if she knew how his heart hammered in his ribcage as he waited for the classroom to fill. For Konnor to slide into her seat and flash that smile.

Was it cheating? Emotional infidelity if he was thinking about Konnor now? Away from the party? If he was equally enthralled with her body and the other stuff? The secrets that Konnor insisted she didn't want to spill.

Don't ask questions, she'd said.

Did Janie ever get caught up like this in thoughts of other men? Irrational, but even as he checked the time on his phone and took one last look at the door—time to start and Konnor was a no-show—the thought of Janie spending her time reeling in any thoughts of other men made him so fucking jealous, he worried it would be obvious. That maybe his eyes were bulging in his head or his fists, balled on his stack of notes, would turn green and start hammering the podium.

Disappointment and frustration coiled with concern in his gut, but Evan reminded himself he could have walked away Friday night. He could have steered Konnor toward someone else, someone younger, maybe. Maybe he should've locked the door, so it would have been a private moment between himself and Konnor. But he wouldn't change a thing. Being with Konnor had been one hell of a thrill, one he had hoped to repeat, but the sex with Janie that night had been fresh and new. Janie had chosen him, even if she'd sought them out because she suspected he was with Konnor.

He swallowed down the worry and suffered through the ninety-minute class. His mind did its best to drag him away from the topic at hand, throwing memories at him like flashcards. Memories of those first gentle kisses out by the pool.

I don't do much kissing...

And the way that deep, throaty laugh of hers had seeped into his blood and made it thick and hot. The way she'd taken control and announced to him that she didn't do slow.

He'd figured today would be hell, looking at her and remembering the feel of her wet pussy tight around his cock. Instead, today was hell looking at her empty chair and wondering where the hell she'd disappeared to and if she was okay.

———

JANIE SIPPED her cab and smoothed her fingers over the open book on the table. Propped at the counter across the room, Evan watched her with a full heart. Their sons were both gone for the week, and they'd already enjoyed one night of being parents at home alone. Last night, they'd grabbed take out and parked in front of the TV to watch *Friends* reruns. They'd stayed up way too late, channel surfing after binge-watching *Friends* for hours. They'd laughed at cheesy commercials, and they'd both ended up a little too absorbed in a cooking show, and they'd climbed up from the living room floor and gone to bed after two, spooning but both of them content with the sweet affection and no sex.

Tonight, Evan had noticed the tiny tattoo on Janie's hip when she'd changed clothes after work. The tiny heart had stirred him; the swell of her breasts over the cups of her bra had revved him up to full throttle. Watching her sip her wine as they waited for the lasagna to bake filled his heart. Tonight, they would make love.

He knew she felt it, too, because now and then, her lips turned up in a tiny smile. She didn't look at him then, but she would fidget and sip her wine.

The light tap on the front door drew his attention and his eyes from his wife. Evan flicked a glance toward the door and looked back at Janie. She met his eyes over the rim of her glass as she sipped and shrugged. Evan tipped his longneck up for another drink.

"I'll get it," he told her as he crossed the open room to answer the door. Mentally prepared to dismiss whatever neighborhood kid was fundraising tonight, finding Konnor on the front porch left him speechless.

"Hey." She swallowed hard and offered a fleeting smile. "Got a minute?"

Evan nodded, sputtered something like *of course*, and stepped aside for her to come in. Dreading whatever she might have come to say—she hadn't just missed his class yesterday and today; according to Janie, she hadn't been at work either day—Evan thought it might be best to keep plenty of daylight between their bodies. He couldn't, though. Her scent enveloped him when they stood together, and his body was back in that den with her, and his head and his heart were still at the pool. Konnor eyed him silently over her shoulder as he pushed the door closed.

"Is Janie home?" she asked quietly.

"She is." He wanted to touch her. Stroke his fingers over her arm or flick his tongue over the back of her neck. But she was back in the skinny jeans and t-shirt and combat boots making her look younger, vulnerable, and way the fuck off-limits.

"Who's here, Ev?" Janie called from the other side of the room.

Evan nodded for Konnor to go on to the kitchen. Janie looked up as he followed the girl to the table.

"Konnor." Janie jumped up from the table. The wine sloshed around in her glass, and a few drops spilled over on Janie's fingers. "Hey. Where have you been?"

"Um." Konnor took a deep breath and cast a careful glance around the room. "Is this okay? Are your kids here?"

"No. Andrew's helping coach at soccer camp for the week, and Gavin's in Oklahoma doing a service project."

Konnor sucked in a quick breath and folded in on herself.

"Sit down." Janie touched her shoulder and urged her into a chair. "Ev, grab her a drink."

Thoughts of everything that could possibly go wrong flew at him as he watched Konnor carefully. She might have already met with someone at the university, though he still didn't truly believe that of her. She could be pregnant, though it would be awfully damned quick to worry about that.

Maybe she had a boyfriend? And he'd found out about the other night?

Maybe she'd lied about her age?

"Ev." Janie dropped into her own chair, still more focused on Konnor than him. Still, her nudge put him in motion. He marveled that his wife didn't have to worry about any of the things he didn't want to think about right now as he grabbed a cold beer from the refrigerator.

"I wanted to apologize," Konnor mumbled. Evan snagged his own beer and took a quick peek at the timer on the oven before joining Janie and Konnor at the table. "Thank you." She took the bottle he handed her, her fingers touching his as she did.

"You're welcome." He nodded as he sat down across from Janie. His wife had already closed her book and pushed it aside.

"I slipped out Friday night." Konnor rubbed her eyes, but

Evan suspected it was her way of hiding. "I shouldn't have handled it that way, but things were a little…deep."

"Define deep." Evan propped his chin in his hand and watched her.

Konnor dropped her hands to the table and stared at him in disbelief. Her small, sharp laugh rang out in the otherwise quiet kitchen.

"Are you serious?"

"You made a point of telling me you were experienced—"

"Yeah." She shrugged and waved his words away. "But not like that."

"What do you mean?" Janie's brows were drawn in an intense frown, but she concentrated on her fingers twisting her glass on the table.

"I've never been with a husband and wife together," Konnor said quietly. "I'm not saying I regret anything about it. In fact, I don't. At all." When Janie wouldn't look at her, Konnor turned wide, sincere eyes to Evan. "God, Janie, pushing you over the edge like that was really fucking incredible."

Konnor arched her eyebrow at him as if she needed him to agree. He nodded, though he wasn't ready to say anything.

"But being with you…after…" Konnor's voice faltered. "Not my thing. So, I slipped out to avoid the…other stuff."

"The other stuff?" Evan repeated.

"Ask no questions," Konnor mumbled what was apparently her mantra, her sword of protection. She circled her fingers around her bottle but didn't pick it up. "Keep it impersonal." She flashed Evan a humorless smile and turned to Janie when he didn't return the sentiment. "You guys weren't going to keep it impersonal."

Janie took a deep breath and scooted her glass away. She shared a long look with Evan as she flopped back in her chair.

"What about work yesterday and today, Konnor? What about Evan's class?"

Evan was startled to realize Janie was hurt by Konnor's disappearing act. He wanted to reach over the table and take her hand, but he didn't want to make Konnor feel left out.

Konnor rubbed her eyes again.

"That's on me." She finally shrugged. "I'm sorry. I just needed to...clear the air with you guys." She pushed her chair back to stand, eyes on the bottle she hadn't picked up.

"Wait." Evan shook his head and pinched the bridge of his nose. "You're leaving? You left us hanging all weekend? And now you show up and say *sorry, it's on me* and you're leaving?"

"I need that to be enough, Evan." She stood, pushed her chair in, and rested her hands on the back of it. "Please?"

"It's not," he argued. "Dammit, Konnor. It's not enough. You told me you and Janie are friends, but you waited four nights to come and talk to her after what happened."

Konnor rolled her lips inward, eyes still on the damned bottle.

"See? You were in that room, too, but you're all about Janie." Konnor flicked her gaze up to meet his, but she couldn't hold the eye contact. "You're all about, Janie. We're in the middle of a three-way, and I want to touch your wife, and you *give her permission*. You tell her to take *whatever* she needs."

"How old are you?" The words were out before he could stop them.

"What?" Konnor drew back as if he'd hit her. Evan felt Janie's concerned stare burn through him, but he couldn't look away from Konnor.

"When you didn't show up for class yesterday, didn't bother to text me or email...it crossed my mind that maybe you lied about your age. And—"

"You thought I would accuse you of assault?" Konnor

yelped, apparently shocked that he would have worried about it. "I told you I'm twenty-six." She dropped her head back and groaned. "Do you want to see my driver's license?"

"No. Doesn't have to be about age," he reminded her.

"Evan." She shook her head.

"Sit down, Kon," Janie urged her. "Stay a while."

"Talk to us, Konnor." Evan shrugged when she looked at him. "I don't know where your other parties happen, but things are different here. Discretion is key, sure. But people are friendly, and there's more to it than sex."

"I don't do more than sex," she said simply. "Which is why it made me uncomfortable to watch you orgasm together."

"What're you running from?" Janie asked her. As if she just noticed the wine she'd splashed on her fingers, she licked them and then lifted her eyes, waiting for Konnor to say something.

Konnor snagged the bottle and lifted it for a long drink.

"I wasn't lying, Evan." She pulled her chair out to rest her knee on it and then slid down the back to sit again. "I've been doing that stuff for years."

"How many years, Konnor?"

"Eleven."

"Fuck." Evan smacked his hand on the table. His chair squawked on the tile floor when he shoved it back and stood.

"Evan." Konnor's desperate whisper was frayed at the edges.

"You were fifteen?" He turned his back to her and lifted his arms to cross behind his head. "Fifteen? Do you know what that feels like for me? It feels like I did that to you when you were fifteen—"

"My stepbrothers." She pursed her lips and then continued in a thick voice. "One was fifteen, and one was sixteen. I was crazy about them...like...I thought they were cool. And fun. Up until then it was all normal. They included me in a lot of stuff. We played basketball together, and Ry taught me how to throw a perfect spiral with a football. Luke taught me to beat all of his video games. They could be ornery, but it was all good."

"Until they decided to rape you?"'

"It wasn't like that," she argued weakly.

Still seething, Evan paced to the counter and turned to find her watching him with those big, innocent green eyes that had intrigued him when he had kissed her.

"What was it like then? Tell us."

"Ev." Janie nodded to his chair. Of course, Janie would want to comfort Konnor, whereas Evan wanted to find her stepbrothers and rip them apart limb from limb, starting with their dicks. He'd cut them off and cram them down their throats.

"I wouldn't have…" He stopped talking as he stalked back to the table and dropped into the chair so violently that it squawked on the floor again.

"Wouldn't have what?" Konnor licked her lips. "Fucked me?"

"Not like I did, no," he muttered. "Dammit, I didn't even touch you. I didn't do anything for you—"

"God." Konnor ducked her head and pushed her hair off her face. "You're a giver. I don't do givers, either."

"Am I supposed to apologize for that? For not being a selfish prick who just wants a piece of ass?"

"They both got into porn," Konnor continued her story. "Plenty of stuff to find on the Internet. Of course, I was curious. I was always with them, so I wasn't about to suddenly give them privacy. I gave Luke a blowjob one day when Ryan wasn't home."

"You should have just been getting your first kiss at that age," Janie said softly.

"At fifteen?" Konnor jerked her head around to look at

Janie like she was crazy. "Luke told Ry, but he didn't…He never asked me. Wouldn't let me. But they had parties…"

"You're comparing fucking around with your stepbrothers' friends to the party the other night?"

"No." Konnor sighed. "But it spiraled. By the time I was sixteen, I was a favorite. Best blowjob. Best fuck around."

"Kon, that's assault."

"They were kids, too."

"Old enough to know better."

"So was I." She shrugged. "And I did tell my mom once."

"And?"

"She said I was lucky that their friends liked me."

"Dammit." Evan rested his forehead on the table and squeezed his eyes closed.

"Look, don't feel bad for me. I'm fine. My stepbrothers were popular. Most of their friends were nice to me. Even at school. They watched out for me, too."

"But they took your first kiss. Your first time to have sex." Janie sat up and leaned toward Konnor. "Your first orgasm —" Janie stopped talking. The sudden quiet drew Evan's attention. He sat up and met his wife's gaze.

"But I'm okay," Konnor insisted. "Eleven years later, I'm fine. I'm well-adjusted. I've got a couple of jobs. I have friends. I've had relationships. I don't do as many parties anymore. The money's nice. But I told Luke I'm just…he doesn't call much anymore."

"Money?" Evan frowned. "What?"

Konnor blinked at him silently.

"Don't make me say it." Her words shook when she finally broke the tense silence. "Please?"

7

S harp pain jabbed his chest when he realized what Konnor was telling them, what she didn't want to say. Evan cringed and rubbed his hand up over his heart. Guileless green eyes watched him seethe with anger. He clutched a fistful of his shirt wishing he could soothe his heart. Konnor's heart.

"Makes it different." She nodded finally and ducked her chin. Evan bit his tongue before he could respond. Hell yes, it made it different for him. He couldn't wrap his brain around the idea that he had fucked a child—

She wasn't, though.

Konnor had just reminded him of that.

Hand cupped over his mouth, he stifled a groan of frustration as Konnor flattened her hands on the table and rose from her chair.

"I'm sorry," she mumbled.

Evan took a quick peek at Janie when Konnor looked at her, too. Pain painted her features, too, her face a mask of regret and sympathy.

"I should have been honest with you before." Konnor shrugged. "I'll withdraw from your class, Evan—"

"I don't understand what's happening here." Janie scrambled to her feet as Konnor gently pushed her chair in.

"Janie, I work parties—"

Impatience flashed in Janie's eyes. She tipped her head at Konnor and arched her eyebrows.

"Yeah, I get that part." She rolled her eyes. "And I get why Evan's upset. But why are you rushing out of here? Why would you withdraw from class?"

Evan drew in a slow, deep breath and relaxed back in his chair. His appetite was gone, dinner forgotten.

"Because hired entertainment doesn't stick around for this stuff," Konnor reminded Janie.

"What stuff?"

"I get it." Konnor turned her attention back to him. "I'm not who you thought I was."

"I don't think you're who you think you are," he answered simply.

"I'm not a kid—"

"No, but you're not hired entertainment, either. Not for Janie or me." He stood, unfolding slowly to his full height, gaze intense on Konnor. "You liked it when I kissed you."

She tried to turn away from him, but Evan moved like lightning to cup her chin in his hand. As desperate as he was to keep her, his fingers were gentle on her face. Blush high on her cheekbones, she closed her eyes, unwilling to let him see her.

"Go ahead. Tell me now that you didn't." He stepped close to her, aware of his wife standing less than a foot away from them. "But you did."

"You know now that I can lie." Konnor's whispered reminder gripped his lungs and wrung them so tight, it hurt to breathe.

"Your eyes don't lie, Konnor," he argued quietly. "Your mouth can do all kinds of wicked things. I'll give you that. But your eyes don't lie."

Konnor jerked her chin from his grasp. She flicked her eyes—narrowed now to control the emotion in them—over his and looked away quickly.

"Evan." She sobbed his name quietly, clearly losing the battle over her emotions. "I'm okay. Let it go."

"But why settle?" Janie caressed her fingers up the back of Konnor's arm. "Why settle for being okay? You deserve everything. Love. Happiness. Anything you want."

"Because this is all I know. I'm not settling. I'm...servicing." Konnor shrugged and stepped back from them.

"Fuck." Evan groaned as he dropped his hands. Still struggling to catch a full, deep breath, he propped his hands on his hips and hung his head.

"They brainwashed you to believe that," Janie argued, but she spoke quietly, obviously hoping to keep the situation calm. "That's not fair to you."

"But it's who I am, Janie," Konnor said again.

"No." Evan shook his head, eyes still on the floor between them. "It's not. It's who they want you to be. But it's not you."

"I should go." Konnor cleared her throat.

"What if I told you I'm not satisfied with the other night?" Evan paced away from Konnor and Janie and stood with his back to them. He rested his hands on the island and prayed he looked nonchalant, because inside he was coiled tight and ready to pounce. Torn between wanting to take Konnor in his arms and make love to her, to show her what she deserved, and wanting to shove his fist down her stepbrothers' throats. The indecision warred in his head.

"What?" Konnor's response was so faint, so surprised, he almost missed it.

Still at the counter, he turned to look at her. Janie

watched him carefully; Evan assumed she was ready to jump in to soothe the angry beast and save the girl.

"You want me to—? Now? But I'm not—"

"No!" Evan shouted. "Hell, no, I don't want you to get down on your knees for me again."

Konnor blinked at him, sexy lips parted as if she was ready for him. But even from across the room, Evan saw the uncertainty in her eyes.

"I wanna touch you," he told her. "I want to put my mouth on you. I wanna make you come apart with my tongue and my fingers. I wanna hear that sexy-as-fuck voice calling my name when I make you come."

Konnor's lips twitched, but she didn't respond. Silence slithered in around them, curling around their shoulders and their mouths and their hands, caressing them all like a lover. But it was hot and awkward and uninvited. Evan held Konnor's stare, daring her to say something or walk away.

"Are you gonna deny me that, Konnor? I want your skin. I want your heat. Let me— "

"I can't," she interrupted him with a desperate whisper.

"As much as I want it for me," he continued, "I want it for you. There's nothing sexier to me than a woman who knows her body and knows how to take what she needs to get off."

He felt Janie's eyes crawl over him, but he kept his gaze trained on Konnor's face.

"Well, then I'm not the one for you," Konnor said simply. Her quietly spoken words were louder than a roar. "Because I can't."

"Maybe you can." Evan shrugged and pushed away from the counter. Konnor drew herself up to her full height as he neared her and pressed close into her personal space. "Maybe no one you've been with cared enough to give you that."

"Evan." She sucked in a quick breath when he leaned in and kissed her lower lip. The soft press of his lips on hers made her jump. Evan waited for her to move, to pull away. To say no. When she only stood there, those wide, needy eyes on his, he used his teeth to tug at her lower lip.

"He's right, Konnor," Janie whispered.

Standing in Konnor's space, with his lips not even a centimeter from hers, Evan felt another stab of pain at his wife's words. Maybe she was only offering Konnor support or encouragement, but part of him wondered if Janie had considered him a selfish lover all the years of their marriage.

"Say no." His gruff voice broke another tense silence. He reached for Konnor's hands and stroked his fingers up her bare arms. Goosebumps kissed her flesh. "It's okay if you don't want to do this. If you want to leave."

Konnor swallowed hard, eyes locked with his.

"But don't you dare withdraw from my class," he continued, his quiet voice stern with warning. "Don't skip to avoid me. Don't miss work to avoid Janie."

She licked her lips, still so close to Evan he could almost feel the heat of her tongue.

"I don't know how to do this any other way."

Evan slid his hands over the back of her arms and over her shoulders. Her shiver gave him wings and made him stand ten feet tall.

"Konnor." He breathed her name over her parted lips and combed his fingers up the back of her neck and into her silky hair. A week ago, Evan wouldn't have considered standing in his kitchen, pressed toe to toe, hip to hip, mouth to mouth with anyone other than his wife. Aware that Janie still stood with them, Konnor's scent invaded his thoughts, and his blood hummed with the need to touch her. To strip away everything, not just her clothing, but all of her fears and reservations.

Evan didn't want to possess her, to use her the way things

had played out at the party last weekend. He ached to take her in his arms and show her what making love *should* be.

She tilted her head. Her soft sigh of surrender lit a trail of fire from his lips to his cock, but damned if he would rush anything. Not again. Not with Konnor.

"Do you wanna stay?"

Evan didn't realize Janie had moved, but suddenly, she was behind Konnor. She cupped Konnor's upper arm and leaned in close to kiss her cheek.

"I'll give you guys some time."

Evan met Janie's eyes over Konnor's shoulders.

"I can't do that." Konnor shook her head. "That's different."

"Do what?"

Evan watched Janie's bright red fingernails slide up and down Konnor's arm and tried to shake the image of Janie's hands on Konnor's flat belly and her small, perfectly round breasts. His cock roared to life, the press of his erection against the fly of his shorts painfully uncomfortable.

"I can't be with Evan and not you." Konnor shook her head. Evan kissed the deep frown lines in her forehead and let his lips linger there. "That's cheating. Making it about me and Evan makes it infidelity."

"Can I tell you something?" Janie still stood behind Konnor. Her fingers continued their gentle massage of the girl's arm, but Evan noticed she kept space between herself and Konnor.

"What?" Konnor turned her head slightly, enough to shift against Evan. He stayed close, his cheek pressed to hers.

"Ev and I've been married twenty-seven years." Janie dropped her hand to Konnor's waist and leaned in closer. "I love this guy. You know how much I love him, Kon. But I couldn't find that release with him. Sex was always…average at best. And sometimes, it was just another thing I had to do at the end of the day."

Evan and Janie held eye contact over Konnor's shoulder.

"The only way I could have an orgasm was by myself or with toys."

Evan saw Konnor wince. "You don't have to tell me this, Janie."

"I know I don't," Janie agreed. "But I want you to know this. The first time Donna invited me to a party, I desperately wanted to go." Janie sank her teeth into her lower lip, eyes locked on Evan's. "But I also wanted to run as far from it as I could."

"What do you mean?" Konnor dipped her chin.

"All those years, I felt like something was wrong with me," she whispered. "That I couldn't enjoy sex. That my husband, the guy who loves me more than anything, couldn't get me off. And then I was offered a chance to…experiment. To play…to see what I like. Of course, I wanted to do that. I wanted to figure myself out. I wanted to find what turned me on. I wanted the mind-blowing orgasms women talk about on talk shows or in magazine articles. With friends over a glass of wine. I wanted more than a vibrator."

Evan skimmed his fingers over the back of Janie's hand, still on Konnor's hip.

"But I was scared," Janie admitted. "First of all, Ev and I are married. So, fucking around with other people. That's wrong. Right? Needing other men…women…to show me what I like…I felt like I was hurting Evan. But I wanted to be that complete, confident woman that Evan finds so sexy. I wanted it for Evan. But I wanted it for me."

"It feels like cheating." Konnor shook her head. "I won't do that. I don't."

"What if I'm with you guys?" Janie offered.

The laugh that escaped Konnor's lips was soft, but bitter.

"Janie." She sucked in a deep breath as she lifted her head to meet Evan's eyes.

"We're adults." Janie rested her forehead on Konnor's shoulder. "As you just reminded us a few minutes ago. We're all adults. And Ev and I are married, but we've had an unconventional marriage for the past year, and I think we're only stronger for the things we've experimented with."

"Just know." Evan's voice was low and scratchy. He cleared his throat. "Whatever happens tonight. You stay. You go home. Whatever. It's all between us. Last weekend is between us. And if you walk out of here, know you're always welcome to come back. For whatever reason."

Konnor lifted her hands and scrubbed them over her face. She laughed softly and shook her head.

"This feels like a dream," she mumbled. "Or an alternate universe, maybe."

"Janie's right." Evan shrugged. "We do have an unconventional marriage. But if we're okay with that, then it's not wrong."

"And if I'm okay with what I did with my stepbrother? What I did with their friends? Then that's not wrong?"

Evan opened his mouth to argue, but when Janie arched her eyebrows, he closed it without a word. He sighed and dug deep inside for the right thing to say.

"It's not wrong in that it makes you bad," he finally told her. "Please don't think that. It's wrong because it's not fair to you. Like Janie said, you deserve anything and everything you want. And if you don't want relationships or emotional ties or whatever..." He shrugged. "That's okay, too. But you deserve to enjoy your body and all the pleasure you can take from me or any other guy or girl or husband and wife or whoever you're with."

Konnor's soft laughter chased a shiver up his spine.

"I don't know what to say." She shook her head.

Assuming her reluctance meant no, Evan nodded and stepped back to give her space.

"It's okay," he promised her.

Hunger flashed in her eyes, but Evan leaned in to kiss her cheek, hoping she believed she truly was welcome to come back.

"Evan." She latched onto him, curled her fingers around his upper arms. Evan felt a moment of pride; he was so much older than this girl he wanted to lavish kisses and tenderness on, but he took care of himself. He knew she felt nothing but hard, solid muscle under her fingers.

She kissed him, her lips eager to catch his before he ducked away again. But once her open lips touched his, she almost shied away. She dug her fingers into his arms to hold on, even when she hesitated with the kiss.

"I want…" Her whisper trailed off, but she nodded. "I want this with you. And Janie. I just…"

When she lost her nerve again, he played at her lips. Soft, dry kisses, his lips to hers. A brush of his closed mouth over the center of her parted lips. A gentle press at the corner of her mouth. The slow, light drag of his teeth over her lower lip.

"Yes," she whispered. "Please."

8

Janie shooed them upstairs to the bedroom, after a promise she would be up in a few minutes. When Konnor tried to protest, Janie argued that she would get the lasagna out of the oven and set it aside, turn the lights down, and lock the house up. While it was all stuff that had to be done, Evan suspected Janie wanted Konnor to be at ease with him first. Konnor hadn't wanted to mess around by the pool, and that was before she had bared so much of herself to them. He supposed she might feel exposed right now, and the last thing he would want in her shoes was an audience.

"I have to confess I'm a nervous wreck right now." Konnor's admission gushed out of her the second they crossed the threshold into his and Janie's bedroom.

"Nervous like you really don't want to do this?"

"Nervous like I really do." Her voice shook. "But scared."

"Of me?" His instinct was to turn the light on, but he doubted Konnor wanted to get undressed and sexed up under spotlights, either. "I'm gonna turn a lamp on. That okay?"

"Yeah."

In the darkness, he moved to the nightstand by memory and twisted the switch on the reading lamp on his side of the bed.

"I'm not afraid of you." She shook her head when he turned to her. "But I'm…I'm used to controlling…this."

"Thank you." He eyed her from where he stood, a few feet away from her at the side of the bed. "For trusting me."

"I feel…" Eyes locked with his, she pressed her lips together and raised her eyebrows. "I trust you. But I feel so… exposed. I mean, I have combat boots on, Evan. Do you really wanna fuck a girl in combat boots?"

He grinned. "Well. Yeah. The image of you in nothing but those boots turns me on. We can do that. But not tonight."

"No?" She tipped her head.

"I'm not fucking you tonight, Konnor." He lifted his hand toward her and waited for her to place her fingers in his. When she did, he gave her a gentle tug. "I'm going to make love to you."

"And what if…" She blew out a nervous sigh. "What if I can't come? And you're bored—"

"I want to lay you down and look at you." He played with her hair, twisted the ends that framed her face and pushed them back behind her ear. "I wanna spread you wide open and taste you."

She swallowed hard.

"I'm not gonna be bored." He dropped his other hand on her hip and gave her a possessive tug to pull her firmly against his erection.

"The Econ professor did it once." She averted her eyes. "I didn't—"

"It's okay," he promised her. "No pressure. If it doesn't happen, it's okay. We can try it again."

Konnor laughed softly.

"Is Janie really gonna come up here?" She looked over her shoulder toward the open door. "Because I can't do this if she's not part of it."

"She will."

He stopped her when she reached for her belt.

"What if…" He took her hands in his again and brought them to his lips. "We started with kissing?"

"You want to kiss me again?"

"I want to kiss you again." He nodded. "That okay?"

Her eyes grew wide as he pressed her up against him again.

"I think you're beautiful, Konnor." He dropped staccato kisses over her cheek and when she stretched and turned to offer him her neck, he smoothed his closed lips over her skin. "Let me do this. Let me show you who I see when I look at you."

He pulled away just enough to look in her eyes. She nodded, her body sinking into his when he reached around her to mold her denim-clad ass cheeks in his hands.

"I like these kinds of kisses." He made a trail of the same soft, simple pecks over her face to the other side of her neck. At the same time, he tilted his hips to rub his cock against her middle. She rewarded him with a soft whimper. "I like kissing your face."

"Why?" she challenged him.

Evan lifted his head to study her for a moment. Finally, he stroked his fingers over her cheekbone.

"Because you're smart," he answered. He grinned at her slight frown. "Konnor, smart women are sexy. I love to listen to you debate in class. You're opinionated, but you're smart enough to be open to new ideas."

"Is that a vague reference to this? To what we're doing?"

He laughed, eyes drawn to his thumb as he traced a line down her throat to the hollow at the base of her neck.

"No, that's your finance teacher telling you he's been attracted to you from day one. Although I wouldn't let myself consider that you would want something like this to happen."

"You fantasized about being with me?" Her mouth gaped open in surprise.

Evan continued his exploration of her neck, fingers feathering slightly over her warm, soft skin. Her pulse beat under his fingertips, arousing a powerful desire in every bone in his body.

"No. I might've ogled your ass in your skin-tight jeans a time or ten, but I'm not a dirty old man."

"I look like a guy when I go to class." She frowned and shook her head.

"Maybe you want to think that. But you can't hide who you are." He dragged his fingers down her arms, eyes jumping to hers when his touch brought goosebumps again. "I love that."

She laughed and rolled her eyes. Evan saw the blush creep into her cheeks again.

"It's because I'm nervous."

"Yeah?" He raised his eyebrows and tipped his head. "Not at all because it feels good?"

"Well." She grinned, the blush raging red now. "How do you do this to me?"

"This is only the beginning," Evan promised her.

"I want you to touch me." Chin tucked to her chest, she lifted her eyes to look at him.

"Where?"

"Evan." She groaned, but she laughed again.

"C'mere." He gathered the tail of her t-shirt in his hands and eased it up over that flat, tan belly he needed to lick. She raised her arms so he could pull the shirt gently over her head. Last time she had taken her shirt off for him, she had been bare breasted beneath it. Tonight, mint green lace over her small breasts rendered him speechless.

"I would have planned a little better if I'd known—"

"Konnor, I love the way you look right now."

She gaped at him silently, her teeth ravishing her lower lip.

Rather than grab her in a greedy rush—his cock strained at his fly now—he traced a line from under her bra to the button of her jeans. Konnor watched his fingers work the button and zipper open and then slide the denim just over her hips.

A tiny patch of black lace peeked at him.

"If I were in the movies, they would match," she mumbled apologetically.

"Yeah, but if you were in that kind of movie, you'd end up dead." He gave her a quick grin, but his hungry eyes roamed back over her bare shoulders and her belly. "Do you really think your panties are gonna be a deal breaker? Because they don't match your bra?"

This time when he looked at her, she grinned.

He flattened his palm on her belly and curled his fingers around her side.

"I'm gonna start here," he told her.

"Start what?"

He took a step back toward the bed, moving his hand to hook his fingers in the top of her panties. He groped for the bed, grabbed the comforter and pulled it back and then turned his full attention to her.

In the lamplight, Evan perched on the edge of the bed and drew her closer to stand between his open legs. She gasped when he slid his hands inside her jeans and cupped her ass again. Evan leaned in closer and sucked her skin into his mouth. Her breasts were soft and light against his head, his face pressed into her stomach.

"Oh, Evan," she moaned softly. Her fingers cupped the back of his neck; the slight pressure drove him lower to dip his tongue in her belly button. "What are you doing to me?" She moaned again and sank into him, as if her knees were weak with desire.

"Do you like that?"

"Mm." She kissed the top of his head. "I felt that everywhere."

"Did you feel it here?" He slipped his finger inside her panties and rubbed up over her folds until he touched her clit.

"Yes."

The heat between her legs was a siren's song, but he wanted to keep her off guard. And control his dick. The last damned thing he would do is blow the second he buried himself in her pussy.

Konnor cried out in protest when he moved his hands, but Evan molded them up over her bare back until he touched the band of her bra and unhooked it. Flicking one nipple with his tongue and nipping at the other through the lace, he stood. A low, sultry moan unwound inside her as he pulled the straps of her bra from her shoulders and tossed it to the floor.

She arched her back, but Evan turned and laid her down over the side of the bed.

"Evan?" She reached for him, but he stroked his tongue over her lips before she could say more. This kiss was deeper, slow and wet, stirring hunger for her in the pit of his stomach, in his thighs, and his cock.

Konnor wrapped her arms around him and tugged at his shirt, but she welcomed his mouth on hers, his tongue sliding over hers in a hot, wet dance. His shirt half-way up his torso allowed their skin to touch and smolder. Needing more, he tugged the back collar and yanked it over his head.

"Konnor." He groaned as he lowered himself to press his skin to hers. "You're so beautiful."

"You don't have to say—"

She hissed when he shifted lower over her and nudged her nipple with the tip of his tongue. Already beaded with arousal, Evan closed his lips over her and tugged gently.

"Don't stop," she whispered when he pulled back.

He blew over her wet, sensitive skin and looked up at her with a grin when her nipple grew stiff and tight.

"Ev?" She combed her fingers up through the back of his hair and urged his head back to her breast. Happy to oblige, Evan closed his mouth around her again and tugged hard. She cried out, her fingers still massaging the back of his head. When he turned his face to her other breast, he cupped her wet skin in his hand and tweaked her nipple in his fingers while he licked her other breast with the flat of his tongue.

She whimpered again, her desperate eyes on him as he scooted backwards over her body. Her whole body tensed when he knelt between her legs and took her jeans in his hands.

"It's okay, Kon," he assured her. "If you don't want me to do this—"

"I do." She licked her lips. "It's just...never..."

"If you want me to stop, I will." He shifted and leaned over her to place a gentle kiss on her lips. "Lemme see you."

She lifted her hips from the bed, anxious eyes heavy on his movements as he removed her jeans and her panties.

"Tell me what to do." Her voice was gruff with nerves.

"Bend your knees," he directed her. When she did so, Evan smoothed his hands down over her inner thighs, delighted with the contrast between her soft skin and his rougher hands. He lifted his eyes to hers when he gently pressed her thighs to the bed, baring her pussy to his hunger, his greed.

The Brazilian made sense, he supposed. Even if she was with guys who didn't want to pleasure her, they would sure as fuck love the sight currently in Evan's bed.

"Evan." She squirmed self-consciously under his admiration.

He slipped off the edge of the bed and quickly kicked out of his own jeans and briefs. Konnor's eyes dipped to his cock, thick and ready for her.

"Not yet." He shook his head when she propped herself on her elbows. Dipping to his knees at the side of the bed, Evan reached for her. Hands under her thighs, he grabbed her ass possessively and pulled her toward the edge of the bed.

"I wanna watch you," she whispered.

Evan rubbed his hands up around her thighs and pressed his thumbs to her lips to spread her open.

"Oh, God." She sighed, her voice jumping an octave higher.

"You okay?" He peeked up at her and held eye contact for two seconds, but he moved his gaze back to her pussy spread open in invitation.

"Yes."

Evan lowered his head and swept his tongue over her seam. Her silence might have bothered him, but he felt her fingers in his hair.

Too hungry to wait, he pressed into her and plunged his tongue into her soft, wet folds. The taste of her arousal on his tongue was a drug in his veins. He heard Janie on the stairs, but he didn't say so. Konnor played with his hair, and though she was still guarded, her thighs had relaxed a bit.

"Sorry." Janie spoke softly as she entered the room. "Had a text from Gavin. Talked to him for a second."

Kneeling between Konnor's legs, Evan felt a pinprick of guilt. He turned his head and pressed his open mouth to

Konnor's inner thigh. Sucked at her soft, sensitive skin and then nipped at her as he watched Janie undress. What the hell did his wife do at the Wild Canyon Estates parties that she was okay with taking her clothes off and going to bed with another woman?

She glanced at him as she stepped out of her jeans. Her skin glowed in the lamplight, and she moved slowly, almost catlike, as she crawled onto the bed to lie beside Konnor. It didn't matter, he decided. Janie had discovered herself in the past year, and there was no denying her confidence now.

She loved him. He didn't doubt her or their commitment.

"Hey." She kissed Konnor's cheek and reached for her free hand.

Evan watched them kiss, but his balls ached with the need to get inside Konnor. His blood roared through his body with the force of a freight train. He imagined burying himself in Konnor's pussy and sliding in and out, pumping them both toward heaven. He gave his dick a squeeze and then reminded himself tonight was for Konnor.

She was still kissing Janie, but he heard Konnor moan long and loud when he rubbed his finger over her clit. She parted her legs wider in offering or askance, her fingers still playing in his hair. Evan watched Janie's hand cup Konnor's breast as he lowered his head again and fastened his mouth as wide as he could over Konnor and suckled. She cried out and bowed off the bed, her honest, intense response driving him wild. He fucked her with his tongue, the textures and heat in her skin making his blood thick and heavy.

He wouldn't make it through two minutes once he got his cock inside Konnor. She moaned his name, though she'd given up watching him and dropped her head back to the bed. Evan's eyes roamed over her pussy, her clit swollen and gleaming from both her arousal and his kisses. He watched

Janie play at Konnor's breasts, Konnor's back arched from the bed silently pleading for more.

He stroked a finger, and then two, over her clit and eased them inside her. Rather than paw at her roughly, he moved inside her with care, looking for the spot that would undo the girl who always needed to be in control. Konnor writhed on the bed, tilting her hips and spreading her legs wider again.

"Tell me, Kon." He kissed the delta between her thighs, his lips brushing the thin line of dark hair that feathered down to her sweet spot. "Tell me where it feels good."

She cried out softly.

"There?" He leaned over to flick the tip of his tongue over her again. "Tell me. Let me make you come."

"Right there," she whispered.

"Here?" He touched the same spot inside her again.

"Yes."

"Come for me, Konnor."

"I can't, Evan."

"Does it feel good?"

"Yes."

"Let go," he urged her. "Janie and I've got you. Just let go and ride it."

"I can't," Konnor sobbed.

"Sshh." He rubbed his tongue over her clit again and breathed deeply to catch the scent of her arousal. "It's okay. No rush. I could do this all night."

She tightened her fingers in his hair, but Evan felt her tense against his mouth.

"Don't fight it, Konnor." He added pressure on her clit and pressed his fingers inside her faster and harder.

"Oh, God," she moaned and bucked up off the bed.

"Help me," he told her.

"What?"

"Put your hand on mine and show me how to touch you."

He regretted it when she withdrew her fingers from his hair, but the sight of her hand between her legs flicking her clit almost drove him over the edge. His dick and his balls were probably the color of the sky in a violent storm, but fuck if he would look away from Konnor's fingers to check.

"You do this part." He licked her fingers, tasting her again, and watched—mesmerized—as she rubbed harder and faster. Evan plunged and dragged his fingers back and forth over the nub of nerves inside her, desperately wanting her to experience the rolling warmth and tingling electric jolts of an orgasm.

She came hard, his name a guttural sound in the room. Her hips and pussy lifted from the bed as she reached for more of him. Hungry for the taste of her orgasm, he pressed his open mouth to her again, dragged his fingers over her one more time to milk the pleasure for her, and then lapped at her pussy. The smell of her arousal hung in the air. When Evan lifted his head to see her face, he saw Janie's lips pressed to Konnor's forehead.

"Ohmygod." Konnor sighed. "That's never happened before."

"You've never had an orgasm?" Janie kissed Konnor's cheek.

"No."

"Not even by yourself?" Janie drew back to look Konnor in the eyes.

"No. I don't do that. I just...it's never been important to me."

"Oh, Konnor." Janie groaned and dropped another kiss on her forehead. "It's important. Of course, it's important."

Evan kissed her belly and rested his hand on Janie's thigh.

"I hope you have more of that for me." Janie sat up and smoothed her hand over Evan's shoulders.

"Of course, I do."

Janie caressed his skin, her fingers dragging slowly over the dip in his back between his ass cheeks. Evan groaned and nipped at Konnor's sweat-slicked skin, but when she cupped her fingers around the back of his neck and urged him to slide up her body, he obliged.

"Condom?" she whispered.

Janie stretched over him, her breasts grazing over his back sending a hot jolt straight to his cock.

"Thank you." Konnor pressed her thumb to his lip. Evan winced but he ducked his head and took her mouth in a long, wet kiss.

"Don't thank me, Kon." He broke the kiss and sipped at her lower lip and her tongue. "I needed that as much as you did."

Janie dragged her breasts over him again as she eased back to sit beside them. She offered him the condom she'd just taken from his nightstand drawer when he looked at her. Rather than take it from her, he sat back on his knees and watched her rip the package open.

Janie rolled the rubber down over his straining cock and then looked up to meet his eyes. With Konnor watching, they shared a lingering kiss.

"I like watching you together," Konnor admitted. "Because you have something I've never seen up close and personal."

Janie pulled away first, and Evan eased over to lie between Konnor's thighs again.

"I wish I could promise you this is gonna be great for you, but I'm not gonna make it five minutes."

"I don't care." Konnor shrugged. "I haven't had sex in this position since the econ—"

Evan pushed her gently to lie back on the bed.

"Enough about the econ professor," he growled as he drove into her slick, wet heat.

9

K onnor moved with him, tightening her pussy around him to milk his cock each time he withdrew and plunged into her again. Her wet heat still new to him, his blood was so hot and thick, he thought he was having a heart attack. His breaths came in short, quick gasps as he rode Konnor; each time he drove harder and deeper, and still she moved with him. Her eyes remained locked with his as they moved, though Evan noticed twice when her lids slid closed in ecstasy. Both times, his name escaped her lips on a delicious buttery moan, and finally, he gave in.

The orgasm ripped up through his ass and his balls. His toes curled, and his inner thighs tingled as she continued to squeeze him, her ankles locked behind his ass cheeks.

He groaned long and loud, his thick, hot blood pounding painfully through him now. Fucking Konnor from behind the other night at the party had been a quick little thrill that had left him wanting more.

Tonight was a wet dream playing out in his bed. His marriage bed. Just the sight of Konnor wide open for him to touch, to taste had been enough to make him blow. Sliding his fingers inside her and learning how to give her the same sort of pleasure she brought him had been heaven. And tasting her when she came with his fingers inside her had driven him over the edge.

"You okay?" He licked the cords of Konnor's neck and then nibbled over her chin.

"Yes."

"Did you come?"

"No." She dragged her fingers up over his back. "But it felt good."

"You're gonna be hurting tomorrow." Janie leaned over to press a kiss to Konnor's belly.

"No. Believe me I've…" Konnor seemed to think better of finishing her sentence. Instead, she bit her lip again and shook her head.

"Still." Janie stroked her hand up and down Konnor's abdomen, and Evan watched her red tipped fingers glide over Konnor's flushed skin. "You'll be sore."

The shape of Konnor's smile changed to demure and a little embarrassed. Evan felt a pang in his chest. He loved this girl. No, he wasn't in love with her. He didn't have with her what he and Janie had built over a lifetime together, but she was special.

The thought of her working another party, blowing some other guy who couldn't take the time to return the favor made him angry.

"It's your turn," Konnor said simply.

"I get to sleep with him every night." Janie shot him a quick peek, her eyebrow arched in a quirky, teasing expression. Evan marveled now at how much his wife had changed. She had always been sexy, but now she understood her power not only to satisfy other people, but more importantly herself.

"Janie." He dropped a kiss in the palm of her hand. "I love you."

Her fingers hitched and curled around his chin, and when he lifted his head to look at her, she was smiling.

"I'm sorry we wasted so much time," he continued. He skated his lips over her inner wrist and elbow and then pressed them to her neck, just below her ear. "All the times we made love, and I wasn't paying attention to what you needed."

She blinked her eyes open and dragged her hand over his side to pull him between her legs.

"My turn," she whispered.

"You sure?" He nipped at her earlobe.

"Well, you need to do something with that erection." Her lips tipped up in a big grin.

Konnor's sultry laugh caressed his back, and then her fingers kneaded his shoulders and his upper arms.

"You're not gonna sneak out of here, are you?" He turned his head to look at her over his shoulder.

"No."

"Because I want you here. In this bed. Tonight."

"You want me to sleep with you guys?" She tipped her head and eyed him suspiciously.

"Yes. I do."

Konnor scrambled to get out of his way when he climbed to his feet at the side of the bed. Janie scooted closer to him and lifted her legs to rest her feet on his shoulders. Evan took a second to thumb her pussy open and massage her thick, wet juices into her folds before driving his cock—thick and harder than steel—deep. Janie rocked with him, bucking from the bed each time he drove into her. With her feet on his shoulders, he had a deep angle, and her tight, wet pussy pulled and squeezed as he moved.

Konnor lay down beside Janie and did what she had said

she couldn't do. She watched them make love, her eyes hungry for every move.

The stars aligned, and his heart froze, and his blood turned to thick, hot lava, and his cock exploded inside his wife. Janie watched his face as she squeezed him and drew the orgasm out as long as she could.

Exhausted, tremors of satisfaction rolling through him, Evan collapsed with them on the bed. He wondered what the tangle of naked limbs and breasts looked like. His cock— though spent and possibly dead forever after tonight—was still semi-hard, and the bed was a mess. The smell of sex lingered in the air, and he figured if anyone else were to see them right now, they might judge them as superficial, maybe even as heathens.

Evan knew better. He couldn't love Janie any more than he did right this moment, and if his heart felt tight and squeezed in his chest, it was because Konnor had taken up residence there, too.

10

They lingered in bed. Satiated and exhausted, they shared long, lingering kisses and gentle strokes and soft sighs. Evan was still taken with the way Janie and Konnor treated each other; they weren't there simply for his pleasure, whether it be watching them or one of them actively touching him. Janie and Konnor kissed and touched each other with what appeared to be genuine desire and tenderness.

As surreal as the entire experience was—because Evan thought this was something completely removed from the Wild Canyon Estates parties—he stopped trying to figure it out. Stopped analyzing it. Stopped worrying that Janie might be upset with him tomorrow or that Konnor might be uncomfortable with them or skip class tomorrow. He didn't think about anyone else. What happened was between the three of them, and maybe it sounded selfish of him, but he finally understood what the sexual freedom had unleashed in his wife.

While he had never had any issues with sex or orgasm—during his marriage or with girls before Janie—he had found

extreme sexual satisfaction making love with both Janie and
Konnor, and he would do this exact night a hundred, a thou-
sand times over, if the two of them wanted it or permitted it.

Once they were awake, they decided they were hungry.
Thoughts of what they had done together blew his mind, but
watching the two of them pad barefoot around the kitchen—
both of them in his t-shirts and nothing else—was just as
arousing. Gathered around the kitchen table, Janie sipping
wine and he and Konnor both working on beers again, they
ate lasagna and talked and laughed about anything and
everything.

Evan was happy to watch and listen to them discuss
books and movies and naturally, movie stars. He loved that
they had all been so intimately involved upstairs and could
sit at the table together and worry about a coworker's sick
kid or wonder about another's blind date. Their laughter was
music to his ears when the conversation turned to a partic-
ular bank customer both claimed to be too eccentric to be
real.

Konnor tossed out a few questions about other students
in his personal finance class. If Evan thought one guy was
shady looking. She was convinced he was a drug dealer. She
admitted another guy had asked her out and sort of nosed a
bit too much in her personal space when she said no. Evan
vowed to himself that he would take care of that. She asked
him if he ever ogled any of the other female students, and
when he said no, both Konnor and Janie stared at him suspiciously.

When dinner was finished, they straightened the kitchen
together. Even then, there were long slides of fingers over
bare skin. Slow, wet kisses that stirred Evan's heart a little bit
and his cock a whole hell of a lot. He wanted to fuck them
both again, but he wasn't sure they would be up for it.

But the night continued once the house was dark and

they were back upstairs in the bedroom. Evan would have been ready in the kitchen, with all the skin on display. But even he didn't want to let this debauchery spill out into the rest of their house. He couldn't imagine having breakfast or dinner next week with the kids, thoughts of fucking Konnor on the table in the back of his mind.

Upstairs, they played again, and Evan was drunk with the constant arousal and satisfaction. He lay in clouds of heaven as both women worked his body until finally, the three of them were too beat to move. They slept together, as Evan had hoped, the two of them pressed to his sides.

It crossed his mind as sleep took over, that Konnor might slip out in the morning. But when Janie's alarm went off at six, she was still curled up on her side facing him. Evan lay for a moment, almost surprised to find Konnor there, afraid the night before had been one hell of a dream brought on by the sex at the Wild Canyon Estates party and his frustration with Konnor for avoiding them since then.

But when Janie hit snooze and the alarm went off again, Konnor blinked her eyes open and stared at him silently. He held his breath—all the worries from yesterday bombarding him again. Worse, he had a flash of a very young Konnor being used by her stepbrothers and their friends.

"Wow." She blushed a bright red as they stared at each other. "It was real?"

Evan grinned when he heard Janie laugh behind him.

"Real."

"After all the nights I've thought about that." Konnor raised her eyebrows. "It was better than a dream."

"You're okay? With everything?" Janie propped herself up on her elbow and slipped her arm around Evan's waist.

"Yes."

"Good." Janie kissed Evan's shoulder. "I'd tell you to come back any time, but we can't do this when the kids are home."

"We can do the parties," Evan reminded them both.

"We can." Janie smoothed her hand over his stomach and cupped his cock.

"It won't be the same," Konnor whispered.

"What do you mean?" Evan lifted his hand and brushed her hair from her face.

"The parties." Konnor winced. "Feels too much...like..." She shrugged and pressed her lips together. "This felt different with you guys. Like it meant something."

"I think so, too." Janie sat up. Evan flipped over to lie on his back. "We'll just have to watch for times when the boys are gone."

Konnor rolled over to her back and then shimmied up to sit and look at Janie.

"You don't have to do this." Her whisper was gruff. "I mean, last night was...perfect. But you guys are married. I'm not part of that."

"Well, I'm not suggesting you move in with us." Janie laughed quietly. "But I like you, Konnor. I think Evan does, too. We can do this now and then."

Konnor lowered her eyes to look at Evan, as if she needed to hear him say the same thing. But she looked away quickly, apparently gun shy after the night they had all shared.

"Konnor." Evan dropped his hand on her knee and gave her a gentle squeeze. "Promise me one thing?"

"I can't." She shook her head.

Janie yawned and climbed out of bed. "I'm gonna shower." She turned back to the bed, though, and gave Konnor the same all-business stare Evan did. "Promise, Konnor."

"It's not that simple." Konnor rubbed her eyes and then dropped her hands to her sides.

"You've let two people who should care about you use you for years," Evan said quietly. "And they give you nothing for it in return."

"The money helped—"

"I don't wanna talk about money. It's not about money, Kon. It's about you. Your smile. Your laugh. And that big, lonely heart inside you."

Konnor sighed and slipped out of bed.

"Don't leave," Janie told her. "Wait for me. We can walk out together in case any neighbors are up and out this early."

Konnor grinned and nodded, but she grabbed her panties from the floor and stepped into them.

"He's right," Janie told her. Evan watched Janie—nude and proud—walk across the room to the master bath. "It was fantastic." Janie nodded enthusiastically. She stopped at the bathroom door and looked back over her shoulder. "But you said it yourself. It was better for you because it meant something."

Janie stepped into the bathroom and closed the door behind her. Evan moved slowly, eyes on Konnor as she dressed. He stepped into the loose-fitting athletic shorts he wore last night when they dined together after being together up here.

"I can't be with you and Janie all the time," Konnor said softly. "How does anything else ever mean anything?"

"You find someone to love you. Someone you love to love right back."

Konnor rolled her eyes. "That ship sailed the first time I sucked my stepbrother's dick, Evan. You know that."

"Do I?" He shrugged. "Because I'm pretty crazy about you. I can't be in love with you, because that part of me belongs to Janie. But I wanted to show you last night that you're so much more than that girl."

"Who's gonna love me, Evan?" She shook her head.

"Well, first they have to see you." Evan tapped her chest with his fingers. "This. Your heart. Your personality. They need to hear you laugh and understand how you think."

Konnor sighed, but she refused to meet his eyes.

"Nobody's gonna see how beautiful you are if you're on your knees all the time, Konnor. Be more than that."

"Wow." She rubbed her eyes. "I need a shower. And I need coffee. A week on a beach."

"You could shower with Janie, but then she'll be late for work." He winked at her. "And I'm short on beaches, but I can make coffee."

Konnor answered his smile with one of her own. She followed him downstairs and watched him move through the kitchen as he did every morning. Once the coffee maker was rumbling through its cycle, Evan turned to her and took her in his arms.

"I hope you know how much this means to me." He kissed her hair and held her tight. "I'm not that guy, Konnor. I'm not the guy to do that. You called it the first night. I'm the guy who shoots the breeze with Bronson the bartender while I wait for my wife to get her fix."

Konnor, arms wrapped around him, buried her face in his neck. Her laughter rumbled up from deep inside, and Evan felt it when she breathed over his skin.

"I could love you," she whispered. "I could be in love with you."

"I know." He smoothed his hand over her back.

"I know. You're the first guy to take the time to make sex good for me, so there's some kind of psychology thing going on there. Some fixation."

Evan felt her lips against his neck as she smiled.

"But." She cleared her throat. "Even…before."

He nodded, afraid to try and speak. Even after the wild night and the explicit sexual things they had done together, this—this moment—felt like cheating.

But as much as he needed to be faithful to Janie, as much as he loved her, he had to give Konnor this one moment.

"I know."

"She's awesome. I love that she's my friend. So generous. Even with you." Konnor rested her forehead on his collarbone. "But I wish just for this one second, you could really love me back."

"Oh, Konnor." He groaned. "Sweetheart, I do."

"It's okay. You don't have to say that. I know you guys are perfect together. You're happy."

Evan cupped Konnor's chin and tipped her head up. Her careful green eyes drew him in, and he floundered there, afraid he would drown. When he smoothed his thumb over her lip, she watched him still. Flicked her tongue out to lick him and then surrendered to his kiss. Bittersweet and so hot it burned him. Long and lingering but over far too fast for his liking.

"I love you," he promised her. "And that's why I know I wouldn't be the right guy for you. And why I want you to stop what you're doing. You deserve more than that. Let the right guy come along to love you the way I can't."

They were at the table sipping coffee when Janie joined them downstairs. Dressed in muted gray slacks and a simple navy shell, Evan thought she looked beautiful and elegant. Certainly not someone who would take part in a sexy, depraved night of three-way sex. He sipped from his mug and hid his smirk behind it. That incredibly gorgeous woman was his wife, and for just a moment, he wanted to gloat in his sheer good fortune.

"Is that for me?" Janie asked hopefully when Konnor jumped up to pour more coffee.

"Of course." Konnor nodded. Evan held his breath and watched the girl for a trace of conceit after their whispered words earlier. He didn't want to look at Konnor now and believe she would purposefully hurt his wife. "You look so pretty."

"Maybe a little more put together," Janie answered around a chuckle. "Although coming undone like that now and then sure feels good."

"Yeah, it did." Konnor's thick voice and sincere eyes soothed Evan's worries.

"Do you want breakfast?" Evan offered Janie.

"Like what?" She turned her attention to him and tipped her head.

"I'll make you whatever you want." Evan shrugged and looked at Konnor. "You, too."

"Mmm." Konnor breathed deeply and then laughed. "I don't usually eat breakfast."

"Well, you should. And you should be hungry after burning so much energy last night." Evan winked at her as he scooched his chair back to stand. "Scrambled eggs and toast?"

"That sounds good," Janie agreed.

Evan set his mug on the counter and squatted down in front of the cabinet to retrieve a skillet.

"Kon?"

"Um." She hesitated and then continued, "Sure. Thank you."

"Need juice?" Janie offered from the refrigerator as she yanked the door open.

Konnor said yes, and they all moved at the same time to put breakfast on the table. Konnor had helped them put clean dishes away last night, so she knew where to find plates and silverware. Janie poured three glasses of orange juice, and Evan diced bell peppers to toss in the eggs.

Once they were seated again, each of them with their own breakfast plate, Konnor giggled nervously.

"Okay, this is...you guys are so chill, I feel like I'm on some horrible practical joke TV thing. Do you do this all the time? Invite single people into your bed? Share meals?"

"All the time," Janie said around a bite of her toast. "Good times, right?"

Konnor laughed, but Evan felt a tug at his heart when she turned her eyes to him. Her smile was fixed firmly in place, but she looked a little uncertain.

"What do you think, Kon? Do Janie and Evan Bellinger strike you as people who host threesomes in their home on a regular basis?"

"No!" Konnor tossed her hands up and shrugged. "No. I mean, I told you Janie's so married at work. And so gushy about the kids. And you're so chill, and you're a financial analyst—"

"Who delivers a hell of a lot more and better than a certain econ professor, right?"

Konnor covered her mouth to hold her laughter and her food in place.

"I think what you're saying." Janie reached out and touched the back of Konnor's hand. "Is that it feels natural. The things we did. And being together now."

Evan studied Konnor's face as she struggled to swallow. She took a small drink of her juice, all the while seemingly lost in thought. Finally, she nodded.

"It does. Everything about being with you both feels so natural."

"Good." Janie looked at Evan. "You're welcome here. Always. But when the boys are home, clothes are a necessity."

Evan laughed. "Our boys would love you. But yes, please, if they're around...fully clothed at all times."

11

Afger what felt like a lifetime, but was more like a week, Evan felt the pressure in his chest ease, and he felt safe to breathe. Seemed like he had been waiting to exhale since the morning after Konnor had spent the night with him and Janie when he had watched the two of them leave the house together. Janie headed off to work, and Konnor was going home to shower and get ready for class.

He'd moved through his shower routine quickly, not allowing himself to remember the things they'd done together. There would be time for that later, and he had no doubt he would relive every precious moment with Konnor and Janie again and again. But that first morning, he refused to give in to the memories. He had to get to class, just the same as Konnor did and just the same as Janie had to get to work.

If he expected Konnor to show up and treat him as if he was simply her professor, he needed to put the sexy, edgy thoughts of her away and treat her as any other student. And he did. He had worried that she might skip class again, that they would deal with the same thing again. That she would decide what they had done was wrong, that she would feel like a third wheel after watching them together.

But she had shown up that first morning—sexy, knowing smile and combat boots—and every morning after that. He was relieved when she was still feisty and outspoken in class, challenging her fellow students to think. She was right; finance could be dry, but often, their conversation steered into current affairs and news items. Konnor never shied away from the debates, though she was never over-the-top.

She was respected on campus; he'd seen that the first time they grabbed coffee together. Konnor had a smile for everyone, and the fact that everyone seemed to know her, that everyone returned the smile and the greeting, seemed to indicate that she was genuine. That everyone liked her.

Once in a while, as the summer flew by, Evan found himself watching the way guys in the classroom acted around her. She had told him and Janie she didn't date much, that she had no interest in dating college kids. But it was human nature for him to wonder if she had hooked up with any of the guys who looked at her with moony eyes. He hadn't asked about her stepbrothers or the parties, and she hadn't given him much in the way of explanation.

He didn't want to know. The thought of Konnor working some asshole's cock or fingering pussy just to turn some jackass on made him see fucking scarlet. He'd kill them if he ever saw it. Still wished he could get his hands on her stepbrothers.

She did go to the Wild Canyon Estates parties with him and Janie, though, she tended to linger near the pool or the bar if she wasn't with Evan. But she and Evan spent most of those nights together, whether they shot whiskeys or messed around somewhere away from any interested eyes. They made love if they found an empty room and simply settled for stolen kisses and caresses if they were outside by the pool or walking hand in hand in the backyard.

Part of him had expected Janie to change her mind about things after time passed and they all came down to earth. But she didn't. He stopped fretting over the things she might be doing behind closed doors, though he was thrilled as fuck when she did those things with him. She still talked about the crazy antics she and Konnor pulled at work, though with them working in different departments, they didn't get to see each other much.

Janie kept the invitation open for Konnor. True to her promise, Konnor was always welcome at the house. And because the boys were around through the rest of summer, Konnor always showed up fully clothed and remained that way until she left to go home. Evan loved her topless and nude and straddling him and under him, but he liked her, and he was happy to have her in his home, as some bizarre addition to his family.

The boys liked her. He and Janie often wondered what they would think if they knew the truth about their relationship. But of course, neither of them would ever share those intimate stories. Not with their boys. Not with anyone.

"So." Konnor approached the podium slowly. Evan loved the charged moments in the classroom when they were alone. She didn't stick around every day. Sometimes, she ducked out of class early, and sometimes she was involved in conversation with one or more fellow students, and she didn't even look at him when she left. But sometimes, she propped her sweet denim-clad ass on the corner of her desk and waited for the room to empty so they could walk out together.

"Hey."

He would never lay a hand on her here. Likewise, she had been discreet, kept her hands to herself, and kept her comments all family friendly. But the eye contact was so intimate, Evan imagined he felt her hands on his skin and her lips open under his when they were alone in the room. An invisible thread connected them, even when every other student enrolled was present. Konnor's sultry laugh and her intense gaze, and sometimes just her heated words directed at other students, plucked that thread a hundred times a class. Evan was thankful for the podium, because his cock was stiff and thick through every personal finance class he taught after the first time he'd had it buried inside her.

"Hi." He smiled. Elbows propped on the podium, he watched her expectantly. Today had been the final exam. He knew without looking at her test that she had done well. Possibly aced it, though he wouldn't hesitate to comment or mark something incorrect if he needed to.

"I can't believe this is over." Voice thick with emotion, Konnor refused to hold the eye contact.

"A few weeks ago, finance bored you."

"Well, a few weeks ago I wasn't sitting there thinking about what it feels like to have you inside me."

"It's just the class, Konnor."

She tipped her head and narrowed her eyes at him.

"You're part of me and Janie now. The class is over, but that doesn't mean we are."

She nodded and licked her lips. "I know." She took a deep breath and reached to touch his hand. A quick look in the direction of the door forced her hand back to her side. Evan watched her tuck it in her hip pocket.

"But…"

"But I like this. Seeing you every morning. Just you and me."

"And seventeen other college students."

"But not Janie," she whispered.

Evan flinched.

"I'm sorry." A small smile played at her lips for a second, but it was gone instantly, and she looked sad. "I love her, too. You know that. But Janie and I have…Ugh. Dammit. This sounds stupid."

"What?" He wanted to touch her, to assure her that he understood what she was getting at. He wanted to remind her that if he weren't married, he could love her—be in love with her, too—but he wouldn't. Not only was it unfair to Janie, but also it felt like stringing Konnor along, and he wouldn't do that, either.

"Janie and I have our time at the bank. With twenty other employees," she added before he could. "But you're not there. It's just me and Janie. And you and Janie…" She licked her lips. "Never mind. This is stupid. You and Janie belong together. I just…"

"I know, Kon." He nodded. "I'll miss this, too."

"You will?" Her hopeful voice carved out a small slice of his heart.

"I will. But at least we see each other. We still have the parties."

Eyes locked with his, she nodded.

"I know."

Evan sucked in a sharp breath when he saw the sheen of tears in her eyes.

"Kon. Nothing changes. I promise."

"I know." She nodded, and this time she sounded certain. She brushed at her eyes and laughed again, the thick, sultry laugh he loved. "Sounds like a cheesy movie. We'll always have Wild Canyon Estates."

The comment reassured him that she was okay. They shared a goofy grin, and then Evan nodded toward the door.

"C'mon. I'll buy you coffee."

"My turn to buy," she argued.

"Save your money." He led her to the closed door and

reached back to usher her over the threshold when he pulled it open. "I'd rather keep you in coffee than think about how you're earning those dollars."

"Oh." She frowned, but her laughter rang out in the hallway. "Low. That was low, Mr. Bellinger."

Evan grinned, but it made him sad that she didn't deny it.

"So. Summer classes are over." She gave him the side eye when they reached the stairwell. "Back to the office? Analyzing things?"

He shook his head and rolled his eyes as they skipped together down the steps. Konnor greeted a few people on the steps as they moved, but she was watching him and waiting for his response.

"Actually, Janie and I are going to spend a week on the beach. And then it'll be back to the grind."

He hoped she wouldn't be hurt that he and Janie had planned a little vacation. The boys weren't joining them on the little get away; it was more of a late anniversary trip, so more than two would be a crowd.

Konnor shot him a peek, brows arched suggestively.

"You might wanna bring your grind with you to the beach, Mr. Bellinger."

"Yeah?" He pushed the door open at the first floor and led her across the hall to the outer glass-paned doors.

"Mmm." She smiled and nodded a greeting at a lit professor when they passed him on the concrete steps outside. "Ladies love a good grind on the beach."

"Speaking from experience?"

"Unfortunately, no," she answered with a sweet laugh. "I wish."

"Okay, while we're gone, you find someone to romance you on the beach."

"Um." Konnor frowned. They stopped at the fork in the path; Evan was parked in the faculty lot and would take a right. Konnor would go left, and they would part company for a while. "Yeah. Where do I find someone like that?"

"Let him find you," Evan suggested. "Just be ready for it. And be open to it."

"I gotta get to work. You can owe me a coffee."

Evan watched her take a few steps, laughing when she stopped and looked back at him.

"Stop ogling my ass." She spoke quietly, but Evan knew exactly what she said. He grinned and licked his lips.

"Kon?" he called when she turned and started walking again.

"All ears," she answered.

He might have said otherwise, maybe all tongue. Maybe all heat.

Probably all heart.

"Come by for dinner tonight."

"I'll bring dessert." She waved over her shoulder, and Evan walked to his car with a small smile on his lips. What the hell would his sons say if Konnor Horton showed up for dinner buck naked with a can of whipping cream? He adjusted his cock as he dropped into his car and drove away, feeling the same sense of regret that Konnor had confessed to moments ago.

As much as he loved Janie, and as often as he and Konnor were together—even as often as they made love—he hated to lose this sacred, shared time together.

12

The sand was cold and wet beneath his feet, but the woman at his side was warm and vibrant as ever. Fingers linked, they walked the quiet stretch of beach, eyes on the setting sun. It had been a perfect day; the stretch of white sand sparkling like diamonds in the sunlight, the sun bouncing off the ocean water that ebbed and flowed. Earlier, the sounds of children playing and squealing in delight had rivaled pop music as their soundtrack.

Now, though, the sounds of the families on the beach had faded away. It was dinner time; he and Janie had this stretch of beach mostly to themselves. Despite Konnor's suggestion that sex on the beach would be fun, they had behaved in public. Through the days, they stretched out on beach blankets and read and napped, side by side. They walked the beach alone when the families corralled their kids and left to find dinner and evening entertainment.

Evan and Janie dined later, finding the restaurants a bit quieter in the later evening hours. They didn't make love on the beach or skinny dip in the waves, but they made up for the lack of adult activities through the long nights that flew by. The first night they'd come back to their room after dinner, Evan had fleeting thoughts of Konnor. He'd imagined rolling around with her, her thighs straddling him and her knees in the sand as she rode him.

Feeling guilty, though he'd already fucked Konnor Horton in every position known and several they'd made up on the fly, he'd turned that part of his brain off and spent the rest of the vacation making up to Janie for what she didn't know.

He wondered now and then if she thought about Konnor. Or if there was someone else she imagined or thought of when they were together. But he couldn't ask. He wasn't sure if he didn't want to intrude on her private thoughts or if he was worried she would guess why he was interested. It wasn't just that he thought about Konnor; he truly wanted to know if his wife thought about other people when they were intimate.

"Do we have time to sit down for a while before dinner?"

Evan cut a quick look at her and waggled his eyebrows. "We do, but we're not alone yet, Janie Bellinger. You can't have your way with me yet."

She snorted and rolled her eyes.

"I'm not ready to go home tomorrow," she said softly. Evan watched her lower herself to sit in the sand. She wore shorts over her swimsuit, but she would still have sand everywhere when they went back to change. "Don't be a wuss."

The dare worked. Evan dropped to his knees beside her and leaned in to kiss her cheek.

"I'm not ready to go back either," he admitted. The week had flown by. Evan liked his life, but who didn't enjoy five days of his toes in the water and his ass in the sand with margaritas delivered and his wife at his side, while they soaked up the sun?

"No?"

"Nope." He shook his head. Eyes on the waves that climbed some only to crash on the sand, Evan felt her watching him. "No. I have a major project coming up at work. Crunching some numbers for a security company, looking to do a major overhaul on their software."

"Thought you liked numbers."

"I do, but I like beaches better." He turned to her, eyes drawn to the curves of her breasts spilling out over the top of her suit.

"Those aren't beaches."

He grinned and flicked his eyes up to hers. "Wanna play miniature golf after dinner?"

"Yes." She nodded, but she eyed him smugly. "But I'll beat you again."

"Maybe I'm letting you win."

She giggled.

"I love the sun," she said wistfully.

"Me, too." He nodded. "Kind of makes all the aches and pains of old age fade away a bit."

"Think the boys are behaving themselves?"

"No." He shrugged. "They're boys. Remember?"

Janie dropped her head back and laughed. Evan eyed her with longing. Age had only made her prettier. He leaned in and nipped at her neck.

"Mmm. Careful," she warned him.

"Will you let me win tonight?" he asked her.

"I suppose you want a hole in one."

This time it was his turn to laugh out loud.

"I messed up. Didn't I, Ev?"

Her whisper followed a comfortable silence. Evan, hands propped behind him, turned to look at her.

"What do you mean?"

"Konnor."

Guilt was a jagged knife ripping through his heart.

"What do you mean?" He shook his head.

"You love her."

"So do you."

Janie shrugged. "I do. But you love her differently than I do."

"Janie."

"I know. I've been fucking other men for over a year. Other women." She sighed. Turned her head away and kept her gaze trained on the water. "I hope my need for that doesn't hurt you."

"I didn't get it at first," he admitted.

"But?" she urged him. "You do now?"

"Yes."

"Because of Konnor."

"No."

Janie turned to him with a look of exasperation.

"Because of you. I wish I had been the one to show you what your body's capable of feeling, Janie. But your confidence in bed now is so fucking incredible, all I can do is laugh. You might be having fun at Wild Canyon, but you're my wife. You always go home with me."

Janie stared at him silently, but her eyes were wide with wonder.

"And I think those lucky fuckers get to play, but I get your love. I get you in my bed, and I get to be inside you anytime we want to be together."

"That hurt," she whispered, lowering her eyes to the sand between them. "When you said that."

"When I said what?" He stroked his fingers over her bare leg.

"When you told Konnor there was nothing sexier than a woman who knew how to get what she wanted in bed."

Evan frowned. "I was talking about you, Janie. I love the

way you know how to revel in that body. I love the sound of my name in your throat. On your lips. When I make you come."

Janie drew in a deep breath. "I didn't know you meant me."

"I love you."

"And Konnor."

He winced and shrugged one shoulder. "I love her, Janie. Of course, I do."

"It's harder to watch you love her than it is to watch you fuck her."

"It's different, though," he repeated. "What I feel for you."

"I know." She nodded and wiped at her eyes. "I do. But it's still hard sometimes to see the tenderness in the way you touch her."

"I would give it all up if she found someone to love her just the way she is."

Janie blinked and then dashed at the tears on her face. Her soft, shaky laugh burned through his skin and his heart.

"Because you love her," she repeated.

"Janie." He groaned and scrubbed his hands back over his head.

"I know. I can't imagine what you're thinking when we're at the parties at Frank and Donna's house."

"Are you asking me to stop? To end what we have with Konnor?"

"No. I guess I just need to know that you would. If I did ask."

"I promise you, Janie. It's you and me first."

Janie stared at him for a moment. Tears streaked her face again, but she didn't bother to brush them away.

"Because she's in love with you."

Evan started to argue, but Janie lifted her hand and touched her index finger to his lips.

"She's never said so," she whispered. "But a woman knows when someone else is in love with her husband."

"I'll tell her we can't see each other anymore," he promised. "Anything for you, Janie."

"No." She shook her head. "I'm not asking you to do that. I don't want to hurt her, either."

He rested his hand on the back of her neck and played with her ponytail. "You sure?"

"Maybe if you just remind me now and then that it's you and me first."

"It's always you and me first." He pressed his lips to her forehead.

"I love you." She leaned into him, and Evan kissed her lips this time. Not just a kiss. A promise.

SNEAK PEEK AT ONE KISS, STORY #4

Legs spread wide, Konnor Horton tugged at the loose bindings on her wrists.

"Don't move." Evan Bellinger's voice was a sexy warning from the foot of the bed. She laughed softly and rolled her head on the mattress.

"How did I let you talk me into this?" She blinked under the blindfold and then licked her lips.

"I think in just a few minutes, you'll be very happy I talked you into this."

"Did you lock the door?" she asked again.

"I did."

"Maybe you should double check it."

"Already did," he reminded her. "Kon, relax. It's just me."

"I know." She whooshed out a deep breath. "I think it's the blindfold."

"Because you don't know where I'm gonna touch you."

"Yeah." She nodded. "I'm a little on edge."

"That's kind of the point."

She laughed again, but the feather light stroke of his fingers over the inside of her right ankle drew a sharp hiss.

"Fresh pedicure?" Evan pressed his thumb into her arch.

"Yes." The word escaped on a moan.

"It's very sexy."

"I'm lying here naked, spread out for your enjoyment, and you're admiring my pedicure?"

"You better believe I'm admiring every inch of your fuck-able body right now, Konnor Horton."

She flinched at the use of her last name. Prayed he wouldn't notice, because now wasn't the time to get into how she wanted more from him and couldn't have it.

"You're not gonna pull out any whips and chains, are you?"

Evan's laugh chased a chill over her skin.

"Kon, you brought the sex toys," he reminded her. "I guess the question is do you have any whips and chains tucked away in that bag of yours."

"But you're the one who brought neckties and a blindfold."

"I'm not gonna hurt you."

Konnor gasped when he turned his attention to her other foot. He flicked the tip of his tongue over the center of her arch.

"Does this song ever end?" she mumbled as the thumping base of the techno beat outside the closed door pounded in her chest. The blindfold made this feel new and exciting, but Konnor would rather be alone with Evan at her apartment.

"Clearly, I need to speed things up if you're thinking about the music and not how I'm making you feel."

She smiled, but it was a weak attempt to put him off. Evan Bellinger made her feel all sorts of things that techni-cally she shouldn't feel. Not since he had a wife somewhere at this party. True, she was most likely with someone else right now playing with her own sex toys. The party theme hadn't thrilled Konnor, but she had warmed to the idea. She had never been one to play on her own, because reaching orgasm had never been important to her. Not until she started this thing—whatever the hell you wanted to call it—with the Bellingers.

"Are you naked?" she asked him now. She wanted to want this. Her body wanted this. Seemed like her nipples had been hard for the last few days, anticipating the Wild Canyon Estates party. Her heart wanted this, wanted this night alone with Evan, while the rest of the world partied outside their locked door.

But her brain wanted to drag Konnor's ass up off the bed and back home. Alone. Her brain had a way of telling her things she didn't want to hear. Like how this was going nowhere. That it didn't matter if she was head over heels in love with Evan or Janie Bellinger, because they had each other, and she would never be first for either one of them.

ABOUT THE AUTHOR

TE Sheridan is the author of thirty women's fiction and contemporary romance novels. She lives in the Midwest with her husband and two children.

ALSO BY TE SHERIDAN